MW01170341

You've Got to Be Shitting Me

Copyright 2023 by Steve Backus
All Rights Reserved

ISBN 9798386919580

Printed in the United States of America

Published by Sprague River Publishing
First Edition—2023

Interior and Cover Design
by Joseph Bergstrom

Back Cover Photograph is from the
Madera Sugar Pine Company, 1922
Colorized by Joseph Bergstrom

YOU'VE
GOT TO BE
SHITTING
ME

Tramp Logging, and Tall, True Tales

Steve Backus

SPRAGUE RIVER PUBLISHING

TABLE OF CONTENTS

I would like to dedicate this book to my very tough mother, Judy McVay, who did what she could with what she had . . . and did it well.

INTRODUCTION
Logging Truck Woes

When I married it was just my luck
    to hook a guy with a logging truck
Now I'm weeping o'er my ills
    not a cent to pay my bills

I swept with a broom—no vacuum to ease
Scrubbed the floor on my hands and my knees
I owned not a dress, 'tis britches I wore
Washed on the board 'til my fingers were sore
Rose out of bed at four in the morn'
Lost so much sleep that I'm wrinkled and worn
Packed hundreds of lunches, caught tons of hell
And to think that into this trap I deliberately fell

My Mother told me of women's sad woes
    the conceit of men as husbands not as beaus
But I didn't listen and in best bib and tuck
    I grabbed up this nut with a logging truck

The grand attitude of my heart's desire
    is after me, you first, if I don't need a tire
It's reaches and binders, fit hooks and scales
    broken rear-ends and motors that fail
There's the gas bill, a tow bill, and a bill from McGee
    and what's left will be grabbed by the P.U.C.

Its a losing game I can plainly see
    for never a penny is left for me
I just left the market with a mere bag of beans
Drooled as I passed a big rack of greens

But there's payments to make and winter to buck
    for my husband owns a logging truck
Bill collectors are beating a trail to my door
    and the sheriff's department is sure getting sore

They've taken the stove and the kids ain't been fed
The old man is hiding under the bed

Now I got a daughter who is starting to roam
Soon she will be dragging a son-in-law home
But my rolling pin is ready and by God he better duck
    if he brags that he owns a damn logging truck!

—*Judy McVay*
(My mom)

THE OXBOW TAVERN

The Oxbow Tavern was located in Humptulips, Washington State, about twenty miles north of Aberdeen and Hoquiam. Hoquiam is a local Indian word that means "hungry for wood"—the white folks were amazed at the trees in the area.

In the Humptulips area, the Douglas fir trees were six to ten feet across, on average, back in the day. Before it was logged, there was more board feet of timber, per square mile, in that area than anywhere on earth. I grew up at the tail end of that era, in the 1960s and 70s; 500 logging trucks a day went past our little burg, and three log loads were common.

The Oxbow Tavern was at the intersection of the old highway and the new highway. Humptulips had a tavern, a post office/store, a church, and seven sawmills!

This was where my mom was raising three kids, as a chainsaw carving single mom. It was a tough place for a woman to make a living, in the best of times.

She dealt with tons of prejudice, sexism, male chauvinists, and downright ignorant jerks. There were also lots of dear, kind, wonderful folk, as well. Jerks get most of the press though, just like today

This would have been about 1973.

Judy had been carving a while and worked hard—she made sure we worked hard, as well. Lightweight chainsaws were just starting to hit the markets, and, being as it was big time logging country, there was no shortage of tools and materials for starting into the carving game, like her older brother. Judy had made some small stuff—totem poles and furniture—but had not landed a big job.

Logging was the lifeblood of Western Washington, and The Oxbow was the local hangout. Kids could go in there, play pool, and eat burgers, but they couldn't sit at the bar—you had to be twenty-one. Seems like the laws at the time dictated that bars had to close at midnight on Saturday, until noon on Sunday, but you could still hunt on Sunday!

You could turn in beer bottles for recycling at the Oxbow, and we never seemed to run out of that resource in the neighborhood. My sister Lynn and I were turning in what we had collected that week, and my mom gave us a ride up to the Oxbow to turn 'em in, one Saturday morning. It was like 7:00 in the morning, and elk season was in full swing, so the woods were alive with the great white hunters. Many of these noble stalkers of wildlife would also get boozed up at all hours of the day and night.

Just outside the door to the tavern were some gas pumps, because in those days they built stuff that way. We were at the side door, unloading the beer bottles and sorting them into the right boxes. It was a few steps away from the main door and the gas pumps; everything was in fairly close proximity to each other.

This big guy comes out of the tavern, gets in his truck with his buddy riding shotgun, fires the truck up, and just floors it! He shoots by me and Lynn by a couple of feet. We scamper out of the way, and, as quick as a cat, my mom grabs a beer bottle and throws it at the truck before it could get fifty feet away. It misses and busts on ground, next to the driver's side door.

The brakes light up, and he throws it into reverse, roars backwards at full speed, jumps out of truck, and pulls out a big hunting knife, and says, "You want to get gutted, you stupid bitch?!"

The "protect your mom," and "fight or flight" instinct were very conflicting for me at the time. My twelve-year-old brain was still processing this situation when my mom grabbed a beer bottle and broke it off. Holding it by the neck she snarled at him, "If you hit my kids, I will string your guts around your throat and strangle you, you big fat fuck!"

He lost the bluff, and jumped in his truck and took off again. We were all looking at each other with big eyes; the whole incident couldn't have taken more than a minute to play out!

The tavern owner had caught most of the incident, and was gonna call the cops. And then he turns to my mom, Judy, and says, "I been thinking of getting a great big sign for the top of this place, maybe thirty feet long. I can get the boards. Do you think you could do it?"

"Hell yes, I can do it!" she tells him.

And that is how Judy got her first big order.

The Oxbow is long gone; burned down. The sign is currently being used to skirt a trailer in the area. I know the guy, and have recently asked to trade a bear for it, just for the sake of nostalgia.

THE BIGGEST TREE IN DOUGLAS COUNTY

Our dear old dad, who gifted us with an older brother 10 years ago (a story for another time), was a source of stories and tall tales that went back to the 1940s. And as he wandered his path, he was always in deep shit, and would dance and twirl his way out of it . . . most of the time.

To say he was a bit of a charming rogue would be an understatement for sure, but he was a sharp guy. It's just that he paid more attention to the devils than the angels . . . "pay 'em in miles" was his company motto. . . .

It was my good fortune to have been able to travel many miles with him, both as a kid, and later, in my early adult phase—where the role had reversed on the child-parent deal. He went with me to a lot of chainsaw carving shows and contests, and would stick around and sharpen saws and fix stuff. But if he had to get something, I would not see him again until I figured out where the local adult beverage dispensary was located . . . and he would be seated there, in most cases, talking to someone he knew, or about someone they both had in common . . . every time. . . .

At any rate, we were heading to Nyal Thomas' Point Arena Californicator Chainsaw Carving Contest, and I am of the mind it was 1998—which was a great year because we were starting what would be a West Coast circuit that lasted a few years.

Early October. Seems like we had a pumpkin carving contest, and most carvers slaughtered their pumpkins— myself included—and Mark Colp won with a lightly-sketched astronaut face.

Dirty Dick From Pistol Crick and I loaded up and got a late start from the island with the grand idea we would make it to Crescent City, California, sometime after midnight. We did, so it was dark as we moved down I-5, south of Eugene. And as we were passing by the very tiny cluster of buildings, known as Curtain— not far from where you can turn towards Reedsport—he pointed out that his mom Jennie had owned a small restaurant on the west side of the freeway. A freeway that had not been in existence, then. He then mentioned he logged the biggest tree in Douglas County, Oregon.

So I gave him a bit of a quiz, because it sounded like bullshit . . . but, like he always claimed, everything he said had some truth in it! He said, "That's why I was setting bowling pins in San Fransisco for a penny a pin!"

Now, I did not make the connection between setting bowling pins in San Fransisco and cutting down the biggest tree in Douglas County, so I simply asked him, "Just how in the hell did you know that that tree was the biggest tree in Douglas county?"

He got a little indigent and said, "Because they measured it!"

"Who Measured it?"

"The Forest Service guys," he said, and proceeded to tell the story of how, one rainy morning as he headed to his little gypo logging operation. The operation was, more than likely, just him trying to do it all with a couple buddies helping now and again, and that day it was just him.

As he approached the bottom of a slippery hill, there was a Forest Service truck that could not make it up the hill. So he offered them a ride, and the nice fellows got in the truck, and up the hill they went.

As they leveled out, and he asked how far they needed to go, they said we are looking for a guy by the name of "Dick Backus" and it's just up the road a bit where he is logging.

Now Dirty Dick Backus, being a quick study in the theater of characters that inhabited his day-to-day activities, correctly divined that this would not be a good day for him if he did not think his way out. . . . So, he said with some conviction that he was looking for that son of a bitch as well, because he owed him a bunch of money!

When they got to the landing (that Dick knew how to get to, but asked for directions anyway), they all piled out. And this Dick Backus had logged over the line some, and took down what apparently was the biggest tree in Douglas County!

Loggers usually have a pretty good idea where the lines are, but, now and again, have been known to fudge things a bit if an especially nice specimen is located close enough to get ahold of it—with whatever piece of shit they had to hook it up to and yard it to a landing. Bummer for Dick that the Forest Service knew all about this particular tree!

He said they measured, and took pictures, and tromped about, and lamented the loss of this magnificent tree . . . and, after a bit of time had passed, Dick then offered them a ride back to their truck and everyone piled back into his rig, and off they went.

He dropped them off at the Forest Service truck, and headed back to the highway leaving them in his rearview mirror. . . .

I was impressed with his quick thinking, and was of the mind that he had to have suffered some consequences for these misdeeds, and said, "What happened? What did you do?"

He said "Oh, I went to the mill and picked up my check, and it was about $4,000. I then went straight to San Fransisco!"

Took him about six months to burn through that $4,000 (in 1955-ish dollars), and he then ended up setting pins in a bowling ally for a bus ticket back to mommy's. . . .

A year or so later, he went to the Forest Service to inquire about them inquiring about him. And, bigger than shit, when he went in the office, the guy in charge was his old boss from when he was in the C.C.C. as a teenager . . . and the guy liked him. (It could go either way with Poor Richard) and the nice Forest Service guy told him, "Don't worry about it; we found another tree."

Dick always thought it was better to be lucky than good.

ROAD TRIP TO PRISON

It would have been fall of 1973, or spring of 1974—can't recall exactly—but I was in the eighth grade, and Kris Barber was in the seventh. We were in the Lake Quin-ault School at Amanda Park, on highway 101, about 40 miles north of Hoquiam and Aberdeen, Washington. It was a single-story building with first through twelfth grade all under one roof. At the time, we lived in the thriving metropolis of Humptulips, about 18 miles south of lake Quinault. So, about a half-hour bus ride.

On the north side of the school, at that time, you sat in your chair in the classroom and looked out the win-dows. If someone pulled up in a car, they could be eye-to-eye with you, at about 15 feet away.

Dick would do this to me once in a while. Often with a couple of hairy hippies he picked up hitchhiking, who he would often put to work for the day, loading shake blocks. Sometimes he'd just to drink beer with them, if he was heading back home to Aberdeen where he lived.

He and my mom had gotten a less-than-amicable divorce, a few years before, and he would sometimes pick me up at school and give me a ride to Judy's. He would get me out of school early, just to piss her off. It worked really well, and I did not mind at all.

They always let me go with him, because in those days it would be fair to say that schools were a little more lax on the whole security situation.

Plus, when I was in the fourth grade, and I was supposed to get swats by the chubby vice principal, Mr. Soth, (for some transgression that escapes me at the moment), I went home and told Dick about it. He said, "Huh, no shit? We will see about that!"

The next day, as I awaited my high noon swats with Mr. Soth's cricket bat-looking paddle—with holes in it—there were some raised voices from the teachers' lounge, where all the teachers drank coffee and smoked "Benson and Hedges" cigarettes, about a foot long. Over the din, I could hear Dirty Dick yell, "Whatever you do to my kid, I will do to you, you big, fat motherfucker!"

His reasoning paid off because I did not get swats. I had to copy a page out of a dictionary instead; something about my dad's grasp of the English language.

So, if Dirty Dick showed up to get me, they handed me over.

Dirty Dick had a "shake claim" on the Quinault Reservation, up towards Queets on the "Cape Elizabeth"—as wild a coastal area as there is in Washington State. Not sure of the process exactly, but he had to have his paperwork renewed and needed the Quinault Indian fellow, who was the owner—or had the rights to the primeval swamp where Dick was cutting shake blocks—to sign some paperwork, and, more than likely, give the guy some money

Dirty Dick pulled up in front of the school window and honked.

The class was amused, I am sure. He waved for me to come out, and said, "Get your shit, you are coming with me." So I went to the office to say that I was going with my dad, and the office folks said "Fine." At some point, Kris Barber entered the picture and said, "I want to go, too." And being as his mom, and my mom were good friends, and Kris was, and I am sure still is, a gifted bull-shitter, they said, "OK, goodbye."

We jumped into the 1967 Mustang, with a three-speed on the floor, and headed south on Highway 101. As we got to Humptulips, he said "I need to get some paperwork signed, you want to go with me? I'll call your moms—it'll be fine."

Sure why not, it was always an adventure with daddy.

So, we went past our houses and continued all the way to Elma, where Dick stopped at a liquor store and bought a fifth of whiskey, then headed toward I-5 through Oakville. He said, "Make me a drink," which meant half whiskey and half water, in a coffee cup.

I knew the routine and Kris piped up, "Can I have

one?"

"Nope only got enough for myself," he said, then he took a long drink and asked Kris, "You ever fucked a fat girl all you wanted?"

I don't think Kris understood the question, and neither did I.

Dick finished off the cupful of whiskey, and said, "Make me another one—we gotta make it to Corvallis, Oregon, by five o'clock."

"Where's that?" I asked.

"It's about an hour south of Portland," he says, and Kris tried to get a drink again, to no avail.

It was about a three or four-hour drive, by the time we arrived at the Quinault fellow's house—it turns out he was a professor at the college in Corvallis. A nice guy, Dick had finished the bottle off and was in fine form. We went in, and they did their business. As we left he said, "I am too shitfaced. You drive."

Gulp!

I had a little driving experience, driving around on logging roads and back roads, but not a highway—much less an interstate freeway, 200 miles from home. But what choice did we have? Someone had to be the grownup. We went first to a liquor store, and got him another bottle of whiskey. He would at least buy us cigarettes.

So, we headed north on Interstate 5, towards Portland, with the intent of returning us babes to our mommies . . . and, as it turns out, he did not call them, and they did not know where we were.

We motored north, and I was a very concentrated driver. I was a large lad, as was Kris, and I did not want to draw any attention to us, because my freeway driving skills were recently acquired. Like, twenty minutes, or so.

As we got close to Salem, the Capital of Oregon, and home of the Oregon State Penitentiary, Dick started talking about playing in the Stonebowel in 1953. "What's that?" we ask. It turns out, Dick and some buddies stole some logging equipment and got caught. Cost him a couple years in "the Joint," as he said.

"Hey do you want to see it!?" he asks.

"No!" Kris and I chirp in unison.

"Turn here, turn here!" he yells, and I obey because I was still new, and we did need gas. We get off the freeway and he is like, "Turn! Go there! Follow that road!" And, as sure as shit sticks to a blanket, we were in front of the Oregon State Penitentiary!

I protested, and he yelled, "Go, go, it's fine—they know me!"

I drove in, and he said, "Just drive right over there," as a big bullhorn blared out, "Stop right there!"

I stopped right quick-like, and a uniformed fellow was right over there, real fast, like he saw it was just a kid driving. I was probably looking scared shitless, (I was) and Dick said, "I have an appointment here."

And the guy said, "OK, but, next time, stop at the big sign that says 'STOP'!" I readily agreed with him, and we went over to where he pointed.

We trooped up the steps, with Dirty Dick calling for us to come along; to come inside with him. He'd had about a bottle and a half of whiskey since noon, and it was getting on to dusk. He could hold a skin full.

We get into what was a lobby, or something like that, and he starts asking about different folks to the person at the desk or window. Don't recall exactly what the reception was, at first, because I was nervous as a hippie at a barber shop.

Dick rattled off a bunch of folks that he wanted to see, and the only one who was there was the psychologist, who remembered him well and always thought he would see Dick again, and was glad it was not in a formal way. Dick asked for, and got, his old much-younger-self mugshots. They gave him one, and we all parted company.

Off to a gas station to fuel up, and the guy putting the gas in was a big bastard. Dick was razzing him some, and the guy was getting a little pissed. Then Dick kind of sobered up, pulled that twenty-year-old mugshot of himself out, and asked the guy if he had seen this guy, because he was wanted for committing petty murder!

The big guy was putting the gas cap on and said, "No, haven't seen him—what did he do?"

"He jacked off, then stepped on it," said Dirty Dick,

and off we go. . . .

Headed toward Portland, and when we get there it was dark, so I get some nighttime driving on the free-way, when Dick says, "Turn here, we will go to Seaside, and take the coast to Aberdeen."

So we drive to almost Astoria across a long, dark, windy highway, and Dick says, "Turn here on a dark drive."

It must be midnight by now, and we pull up to a lit-tle house. He says, "We will stay here." He gets out and beats on the door, and this female voice bellows out from within, obviously having just woken up, and sounding pissed. "This better be good!" she yells, as she opens the door. She sees Dick, shouts out his name, and gives him a big hug.

"Got any whiskey?" he asks.

"Sure do. Come on in." She and her husband sat up with him, telling tales, and Kris and I sacked out on the couch.

We get up, and continue our journey—I continue to drive, because Dick was having whiskey for breakfast. It took hours to get from Astoria to South Bend, where Kris' dad lived, and Dick thought it would be fun to stop and say "hi," so we did.

I don't think Kris' dad was all that impressed with the fact that Kris got out of school and went with us, so, when we left, he pulled us over and took possession of his son.

Down one man, we kept on to Aberdeen, and I then found out that Judy didn't know where we had been, and to say she was pissed would be an understatement. Kris' mom, Sue, would have cut Dick's sacks off, if he'd showed his face.

He did not pull a stunt like that again, and was banished to Alaska before long, and that is a story in itself . . . for another time.

I was 13, when this happened.

Dirty Dick's Theme Song

I'm Dirty Dick, from Pistol Crick
It takes a good man to whip me
And it don't take him long
I'm ruff and tuff
And hard to bluff
I was born in a whorehouse
And raised like a slave
Fighting and fucking is all I crave
Kicking out widows
Breaking down doors
And loving them pretty little whores

THE FOREST PRIMEVAL

Most of the things that go awry for me personally are my own doing. Usually by business not attended to in the past days, weeks, months, and, in some cases, years. Princess NoNo is unafraid to point this out, in many relevant cases (there's plenty to choose from!)

At any rate, the memory dredge has been churning along, and these dark mornings, when the sun is late to work—combined with the "Can't carve until I can see" (not a big fan of carving under lights, but I will)—means I sit at the electric box and write.

I was recently reminded of some of my very earliest exposure to the cedar block industry, and my peripheral involvement. I'm reminded, because I have some recently acquired brothers and sisters, and nephews and nieces—plus my own kids—who are fascinated that I made it through childhood in one piece, compared to their raising.

We are talking, of course, about Dirty Dick Backus, who never won a father of the year award, but made us all natural-born survivors—because he was one of the greatest survivors I knew and a likable rogue that touched the lives of many people. Sometimes, they did not want to be touching lives with him, but he could make that tough when he would show up on the porch with a couple bags of groceries, and a gallon of wine.

My thought/memory (maybe a dream) that was upon me, this morning when arising, was this:

When I was about seven or eight, when he and Judy were still together (she wised up), and we lived in Aberdeen, Washington (1967-ish), Dick got fired from his log truck driving job. So, he started cutting shake blocks up on the Cape Elizabeth, which lies on the northern coast of the great Quinault Reservation, mid-coast of Washington State, and is better than an hour's drive north of Aberdeen. Nice view on the commute.

I was to go with him to work at the time, even though I was a kid, so I could walk out for help if he got hurt—it was very remote. I was to go to George Bertrand's house, because he was closest, and he and his wife Helen lived right on the cliff, if memory serves, a few miles south of Highway 101, on logging access roads that ran down the Pacific Coast of the Rez.

George was a Gray's Harbor Deputy Sheriff, as was his son, Mike Bertrand. In fact, after I had become a teenager, George gave me my first traffic ticket, and Mike gave me my first "minor in possession" ticket. I have nothing but fond memories of both.

But I digress. Dick gathered up his cedar, to make

shake blocks, which he then sold to mills that went on to split and saw them into the nice bundles of red cedar shakes or shingles you see in Home Depot, these days.

In the 1960s—before environmental considerations were even a thing in the logging industry, and helicopter pilots were still being trained in Vietnam—the way they did it, in many cases, was to get a big bulldozer and hook them logs up, and drag them out to a landing, or a place on the road, in which to split them up into blocks and load them on trucks to haul to the mill.

Dragging them out was a job that one guy could do in most cases; find a log and get the 'dozer up by it, hook the choker up, and then winch it out to where you needed it. These "Shake Claims" were mostly logged-over sections that were sold to shake cutters, who would come and get the downed wood that the loggers left be-hind, and whatever buried logs they could drag out.

And there were buried leviathans, I assure you. Often, he would drag a cedar log out of the ground that would have the stumps of the freshly logged trees that had grown on top of the buried log; with big roots that grew around it. And those trees that they had cut down were often, four or five feet in diameter.

He would cut the buried log (seemingly cutting into the ground), to a length the 'dozer could pull out (a TD-24 International, I believe—don't think he ever paid for it), then he would pull them up to the landing, and I had the coolest tunnels in the world to play in! What a place for a kid to play: In and around giant trees, old growth stumps, bulldozers, big chainsaws, and rough characters that seemed to flock to Dick like moths to a flame.

I got kinda windy with the backstory, but those who may have known "Poor Richard" may know the area I describe. And some may not know what the hell I am talking about—for them: Get a map.

Imagine, if you will, a hot August afternoon, on the Western Olympic Peninsula, and Dick and I are at the site. He is worried they will shut the woods down, because of the fire danger, and he would not be able to make any money for what could be weeks. So he was in a hurry to pull logs out of the earth (you mined them), stack them up on the landing, and cut them up into blocks, so as to have some money.

I was useless as a helper at that age, so I spent most of my time exploring, or feeding our lunch to these really cool jaybirds that would take stuff right out of your hands! That really would piss him off.

On this particular day, it was very hot out, so I found some shade and read comic books, and Dick stripped right down to his shorts and got that big 'dozer out sowing destruction in the underbrush. That part of the world is a giant swamp, in which the Forest Primeval had ruled supreme for a million years and a day, and it would demand a sacrifice now and again. This would be one of those days.

Often a curse is accompanied by an answered prayer,

but I suppose that would depend on one's perspective.

On that hot day, as I read and played, I could hear the 'dozer in the distance, snapping and cracking its way along, and Dick had pulled several logs up to the landing, and he would say "it's as hot as a pawn shop pistol," and back into the brush he would go, to pull another big cedar log out of the ground. I had found the perfect shade spot under a big old stump, and was all nestled in with the smell of the earth and decomposing stump as my den mates.

Don't recall the comic book; probably Sgt. Rock.

At any rate, at some point, I could not hear the 'dozer, and there was a loud screaming of indistinguishable words and curses coming from the direction Dick was working, and my little kid heart went beating kinda fast. Off I went over the cat trail of broken logs and trippy brush, towards the wailing.

As I came into sight of Dick, he was on his knees in his white underwear screaming and shaking both of his hands at the sky, tears pouring down his face as he shouted very passionately, "WHY ME, GOD?! WHY ME?!"

Behind him, was that giant bulldozer, buried up to the top of the tracks, stuck firmly in the gelatinous mess of his own making. It was firmly and deeply stuck!

He knew he would have to hire someone to truck another 'dozer over there, to winch it out, and it was going to cost him, and he wasn't going to get any more wood on the landing, and he was not going to make any money now, and all because God didn't like him at the moment. It seemed he only believed in God when being dealt an unfair blow to his plans.

The Forest Primeval had extracted its stern tax

As mentioned earlier, the balance between a curse and answered prayer is often simultaneously delivered and I had been praying that we could go home, and there we went!

Gotta go home now, was my thought at the time.

DIRTY DICK BECOMES AN ALASKAN

When young Richard was a mere 15 years of age, they lived in the metropolis of Drain, Oregon, or up the Smith River, to be more precise. His mom Jennie gave him $80 to go to the dentist in town, and he said he walked out that door and did not see his mom for two years!

He lit out for Coos Bay, Oregon, worked in a logging camp for a bit, then lied about his age and joined the Navy.

It was 1945, and the Big One was still going. Dick was in the Service at a time that qualified him as a vet, and that helped him out tremendously, later in life, when he leaned on the Vet Hospital for care.

When he finally returned home, enough time had passed that the F.B.I. showed up at the door to ask him why he had not registered for the draft!

He answered the door in his uniform, and they cleared things up pretty quick.

At any rate, let's flash forward to 1973 or 74, and

Dick was living in Aberdeen, Washington, on Rice Street, and had gotten in on the King Crab fishing at a time when it was just starting to grow. While on the high seas, he was tossed around pretty good and hurt his back.

Back in Aberdeen that spring, he ended up getting a settlement. And when he hobbled up to Seattle, to the insurance offices, and picked up the money, he received $14,000 and asked for a $10,000 cashier's check, then a $4,000 check he could cash right away.

"No problem, Mr. Backus," said the nice insurance fellow. "And would you like me to go downstairs with you, to vouch for you at the bank?"

Dick said that would be great.

Everything went splendidly at the bank, and Dick got a big wad of cash all tucked away, and the nice insurance man stuck his hand out and said, "Thank you, Mr. Backus, and have a good day."

Dirty Dick Backus hung his cane on the guy's wrist and said, "You bet your ass I will!" And he walked out that door with absolutely no clue that he would be a full-time Alaskan resident, in less than five months.

He had a blast. . . .

It was a good summer for us kids, for sure, even though he wouldn't give Judy a dime, because he could be a touch vindictive.

He burned through it pretty quick, and was holding court at the Smokeshop in downtown Aberdeen. It was fun, but bled the money off very fast. I could buy Bull Durham from Tinker Ashlock then, at the age of 13, and I spent a lot of time waiting for Dick at that place.

By July, Judy was fed up with his bullshit, and took him to court for child support—which was not as big a deal then as it is now (in a legal sense). He was playing the part but she was actually raising the kids; he was Santa Claus when we went to stay with him occasionally, but Judy was the parent—it was she who administered justice. Dick's advice ran more towards "don't get caught!"

This ended up in court, of course, and the judge asked Dick—who was on the stand—if he spent $14,00 and did not give this woman raising his kids any money at all?

Dick reared back and put his new boots up on the rail, and said, "Nope, Your Honor, not a dime!"

It might have been the boots on the rail that got him two weeks in jail for contempt, but the arrogance about the money could have contributed to it, I am thinking.

His mom, my grandma Jennie, got Judy to get him released, and he took off for Ketchikan, Alaska, because he could get a job there. And also because he was very much a part of the itinerant tramp logging culture of the times.

He stayed in Alaska until our brother Boaz turned 18 and the coast was clear.

THANKSGIVING ROAD TRIP

The memory dredge seems to be running full tilt on a rainy morning, and I drift back to a childhood memory of 1968; when we were supposed to go to my mom's mom's place in Spokane, Washington. Grandma's place was a warm, normal house that always had the power on and the phone worked.

It was a day-to-day struggle for Judy, in general, and our dad "Dirty Dick From Pistol Crick" was a bit of a rascal, who was not a very consistent family guy. He often chased big dreams that most often met with disappointment—but every once in a while, he would pull a rabbit out of his hat.

Dirty Dick had been in pursuit of a big cedar claim up on the Cape Elizabeth, located on the northern corner of the Quinault Indian reservation. the Quinault Rez was a thirty mile triangle, that stretched from Queets to Tahola, on the Washington Coast, then to the foothills of the Olympic Mountains at Lake Quinault. Most of it was a primeval swamp, full of the most magnificent old growth cedar ever seen on the planet!

He had been a tramp logger for twenty years and was going to go cutting shake blocks on a grand scale. And once he got all his paperwork lined up, he could get some up-front money to buy a big bulldozer and go to work. If memory serves, it was a TD-24 international.

That's how you did it in those days, my friends, you plowed those large machines through the brush, to find those incredibly big logs buried in the ground. Then you dug a choker hold around them and pulled them, groaning, creaking, and cracking, right out the good earth and up to the landing, to be bucked into shake blocks and hauled to a mill.

That was the beginning of a nice hand-sawn shake or shingle you take out of a nice neat bundle.

But I digress.

We had been waiting for the big provider to return to the homestead, and were excited to see him because we had no money and had not gotten anything for Thanksgiving, food-wise; because we were going to Grandma's. Plus, Judy had no money; she always worked hard, and had a lot of different jobs in those days, but nothing approaching financial security.

I recall her complaining about a bartending job at the Wigwam, just north of Hoquiam, because the man who worked with her got a dollar more an hour, while she swept, stocked the bar, cleaned, and did pretty much everything except chew Copenhagen. And he sat on his ass and read the paper most of the time—didn't seem fair then, and it doesn't seem fair now!

Keeping in mind Daddy was an inconsistent source of money, and that the labor market was stacked against her, one can see why she fell so hard for the chainsaw carving game. I, for one, am very happy about it.

To this day, when asked how I got started, I reply to the person asking that I am a second-generation carver, and they always say, "Oh did you learn it from your dad?"

I always delight in the momentary look of confusion when I say, "Nope. Learned from my mom!"

Like I said, the beatings paid off. . . .

Judy's brother Mike had been carving since the late 1950s, so it was on the carving radar, and her life circumstances were ripe for independence. But that's another story for another day.

Nothing like a cold, rainy, gray November day to set out on a road trip across the state. And we had waited all day on the Wednesday before Thanksgiving for Dirty Dick to return.

He had left the day before, to get his front money and we had not heard from him. Judy was getting a little antsy to go, or at least get us something to eat, as the day went on.

Wednesday night came and the macaroni and cheese was distributed evenly. This was long before the Kraft boxes, so it was noodles, cheese, and those gross tomatoes out of a can. Hunger being the best seasoning, we tucked in and went to bed early, with no sign of Dirty Dick.

Early on Thanksgiving morning, daddy rolled in, still shitfaced from the night before, and puked up a big Chinese dinner next to the truck, which had not sat well.

He then came in the house and promptly passed out on the couch. Judy was pissed, to say the least, and muttered something about smothering the bastard with a pillow. Lynn and I were delighted to see him, Boaz was but a toddler, and we kids assumed all was well. Just another normal day at the Backus house.

Judy said, "Get your clothes on, we're going to Grandma's." In the Time Honored Tradition of many wives of drunk husbands, she rolled him for his wallet and keys, got us kids loaded in the truck, and off we went to Spokane to Grandma's!

As we pulled out of the driveway, I could see that all the neighborhood dogs were lapping up the sizable puddle of predigested Chinese food that Dick had provided them on Thanksgiving Day. In Humptulips in those days, you did not need to have a dog, you just needed a bag of dog food and you could have half a dozen dogs.

I suppose the lesson I have carried from that fine day, is to truly be thankful for whatever you have, because some have far less. Thank God for strong women; they bind it all together.

Not necessarily a chainsaw carving story, but, in a

way, it is, because if things had been easy for her she might not have taken to the saw so hard! Then where would we be?

Comfort breeds complacency; strife and hardship build character. Could be why her kids have so much character.

Rain's letting up; gotta go eat turkey.

1973 GAS PUMPS

I recently came across a picture of Dirty Dick with some of his Alaska buddies: Freddie Broulette from Haines, and John Tanner from Juneau. Spring of 1987 it was, and I was brand new in my place, where I still am today. They all moved in with me, with a couple of campers and tents for the spring and summer. Listening to them talk about their Alaskan escapades from Fairbanks to Kodiak was worth the rent that no one paid.

As we drank wine (yes it was Carlo Rossi) and ate whatever creative mixture Rotten Richard boiled or fried up—Dick was a great cook and an enthusiastic eater, it was more than likely why he lived so long; if you wanted him to pass out and go sleep just give him a sandwich or doughnut; worked every time—the stories they told as we sat and boozed it up were just great. And they will spill out at some time, but not now. They were all triggered when I found this picture. Sigh, so many stories . . . thank the Lord for spellchecker. . . .

At any rate, childhood driving lessons seem to be a central theme of late, and most of the relatives were in the club at one point or another. When my Uncle Pat McVay was Dick's fourteen-year-old brother-in-law in 1964, we lived in Seaside, Oregon, or Gearheart, to be more precise, and we were in the process of moving to Aberdeen, Washington. Dick was sending Herman Silvers, a logger buddy who was an Indian from Canada, with a pickup truck full of stuff up to Aberdeen, with Young Patrick tagging along. Just as they were getting ready to go, Dick said, "Let Pat drive."

Pat told me that Herman was terrified the whole way to Aberdeen.

Dick had bought a logging truck and was hauling logs up in Grays Harbor. He got a ticket at the scale house for being overweight, and it was big enough to piss him off so much that he threw the title of the truck at the cop and said, "I didn't pay that much for the truck! Keep it!" And he started walking down the road.

The cop let it pass because it was a first offense. (Doubt it was.)

The log truck phase lasted a couple of years and inspired my mom to write the introductory poem about log truck drivers and their long-suffering wives. It's a classic.

Would have been 1964 or '65. We lived on B Street in Aberdeen, when I started kindergarten. At any rate, getting everything transported was an ongoing process. The bridge over the Columbia River was being built at the time, so we took a ferry from Washington to Oregon and back. I can recall seeing the bridge under construction from the ferry deck, and that is why and how we moved to the hungry harbor.

Now for the main feature.

*   *   *

Would have been the summer of 1973, and Dick and Judy had been split up for a few years by then, and they had developed a bit of a routine for dividing the kids up in the summertime. We would often go into Aberdeen and stay with Dick on Rice Street, where he lived in a house his mom owned. He was not that good at paying rent, so it was well-suited to his lifestyle.

It wasn't baseball and picnics with daddy—it would be fair to say he could have benefited from some parenting classes. During one two-week period, he bought some cheap movie tickets at the D and R Theater in Aberdeen. They were good for two matinees a day, during weekdays, so Lynn, Boaz, and I saw two movies a day for five days a week, two weeks in a row, as he sat in the Smokeshop, about a block away, drinking whiskey. It was a 24-hour restaurant/bar hub of activities, plumb full of sinners and he was right at home.

When the movie was over, and we came to get him out of the bar, he would send us back to watch it again. "Don't want to waste them tickets," he would say. One week was *The Sting* with Paul Newman and Robert Red-ford, and the next week it was *Little Big Man* with Dustin Hoffman, so at least they were good movies.

At any rate, he was cutting shake blocks on the Rez that summer, and the movie thing must have been during the fire danger shutdown, and eventually, he had to go back to work and decided to buy a block-hauling truck that was bigger than the one he had, and he found one in Taholah. (That's the tribal headquarters for the Quinault Tribe, in the southern corner of the Quinault Nation land.)

I don't recall what type of truck, maybe International, but it had a big long bed and would haul four or five cords of those beautiful red cedar shake blocks.

Dirty Dick's good buddy Dick Robbins was a dynamo of energy, himself; he was the typical WWII veteran/logger, get-r-done, kind of guy that were as common as rain in that country, at that time. He only had two fingers on his left hand—the little one and the next one over—he left the rest of his fingers and thumb in "the bite of the line." Like most loggers, he called any disability a "pain the ass."

He was a submarine guy, in the war, and he and Dirty Dick could consume copious amounts of whiskey, as we will soon see.

On the day he was going to pick up his truck, his buddy "Little Dick" as Dirty Dick called him, had shown up in the morning and they asked if I wanted to go.

I said, "Sure, can Tony go too?" (he was the kid that

lived across the street from Dick's place in Aberdeen, about the same age as me.) Tony Naskota, or something like that. He still lives there, I hear. At any rate, we jumped in the little Datsun "four on the floor" station wagon, and off we went up to Tahola to get the truck. It was a sunny morning and nice and clear with lots of blue sky.

After getting the truck, they were trying to decide which way to take the truck over to Highway 101, and leave it at the log scale place, north of Lake Quinault. Rainier's scale shack, if memory serves. The reason is that he needed it up towards Queets, which is located smack dab in the center of the Olympic peninsula, or close to it. Then the truck would be closer to where it needed to be, and they could pick it up the next day, on their way north to cut shake blocks. Seemed like a simple plan; we could be back in Aberdeen by dinner.

Did not go as planned.

There were two ways of getting there from Tahola; one way was to go back south on 109 a bit and cut across to Highway 101, on the cutoff road from Moclips to Neilton, which is nice and open, somewhat paved. It enters highway 101 about 15 miles, or better, south of where they wanted to park the block truck overnight, then return to Aberdeen by the highway. They could pick up the block truck on the way north, the next day. Dirty Dick would drive the big truck and Dick Robbins would drive the Datsun station wagon with me and

Tony riding in the car with Dick Robbins. This option would have been successful in my opinion, with the high hill of time to view it from.

The second option was to cut across the Quinault Reservation. As the crow flies, it was less distance. By ground transport, it was altogether different.

The first step was to get across the nice big bridge spanning the Quinault River, built by the State because there were plans on having the Coastal Scenic Highway System go right up the coast. The bridge was built, and the Tribe had second thoughts and said, "No thanks; don't want the headache." So there is a great bridge over the Quinault river.

Once over that bridge, one must know how to get across the giant maze of logging roads and find the Raft River bridge, which would then get you on the north side of the Rez. It would be possible to get to the appointed parking place on highway 101 and arrive early at that. We could probably avoid 101 altogether, and land at the scale shacks themselves.

No map, just a fair amount of experience cutting blocks in that country gave them plenty of confidence in the Lewis and Clark department. You can guess which way we went.

Dirty Dick went to the back of the Datsun, popped the hatch open, and grabbed a bottle of whiskey and a water jug. "Steve, you drive the Datsun, and, Robbins, you hop in the truck with me."

Tony and I looked at each other and went *WTF?* As Dirty Dick walked away, he said over his shoulder, "Try and keep up."

I knew how to work a clutch, a bit so I was experimenting with it a little bit, and Dick just took off in a cloud of dust, heading towards the big bridge. I took off rather clumsily but heading in the right direction. In the next hour, I became fairly proficient in the clutch and braking system of mid-60s Datsun station wagons. It helped me a lot of months later, during my freeway introduction.

Those fellas drove with confidence, and we followed at a good clip with less confidence, but couldn't let up because he never slowed down. And, after what seemed like a long time, and a couple backtracking episodes we ended up exactly where we were supposed to be.

Seems like it was early afternoon when we arrived at the scale shack. I was all pumped up after the big race and was ready to get back to town and tell everyone about the big drive.

But the Dicks were enjoying their firewater, and it was still early in the day, so they thought we would go up to the Kalaoch Lodge, well north of where we were, and in the wrong direction. But they had a nice bar there, and that's where we were going. For some reason, we took the big truck, got ourselves stuffed into it, and off we went.

I was twelve, maybe just turned thirteen, and had

some caretaker experience with these two wild-ass log-ger types under my belt. Maybe I did not realize it at the time, but my powers of observation were being devel-oped at an accelerated rate, and scanning for danger and escape routes became second nature. Useful skills that I still use. If you were in a room with these guys it was al-ways good to know if the door opened in or out. . . .

We rolled into the Lodge, and they parked the truck right in front and gave us a couple bucks for the little, expensive tourist store that had its gas pumps in front of it. In those days, it was the Chevron brand of petroleum products.

It was all pretty tight quarters. The store had pop and old candy, and some Hostess cherry pies that would have worked as hockey pucks. The Dicks went upstairs, to what could be considered a classy place, in those days, and it is probable that it still is. They were only gonna have a couple of drinks, and head back to town. Tony and I explored the beach and the grounds. It was a very cool place, and surrounded by some wilderness that was jungle.

We grew bored after a while and went to check on our responsible adults.

They were in the process of getting kicked out of the bar, and Dirty Dick was telling the bartender that they were serving watered-down whiskey, and he had been kicked out of better places than this isolated shithole. The bar staff seemed a little tense, as the ruffians made their exit.

It was getting on to dusk, and I was thinking about food. It sure looked like we were not going to get anything at that place!

They were convinced that the bartender was a fruit, and I supposed he liked apples.

It was getting on to dusk, and as we walked to the flatbed, with them muttering in indignation, we walked by a line of bicycles from some "bike along the coast" types. In the early 1970s, the bike craze was catching on, and packs of those creatures lined the narrow Highway 101. Logging truck drivers despised them as traffic hazards. The whole Hippie vs. Redneck thing was starting to bloom at that time, as well.

"Oh look at this," says Dirty Dick, and grabs a bike and throws it on the truck, while saying, "One of them hippies can hitchhike!"

I said, "No, don't do that."

No good could come of it, was my thought, but to no avail, and into the truck we went. He fires it up, backs out, and is headed out by going through the little passage between the little store and the gas pumps.

He was moving at a pretty good clip, as the front corner of the big truck bed, just behind the driver-side door, caught the far gas pump and plucked it off its base like a rotten tooth!

The momentum was such that the rear wheels of the truck bounced over the gas pump with a lot of noise and quite a jump in the air. As we settled back to earth and came to a stop, Dirty Dick was set to take off again, but the geyser of gasoline spurting thirty feet into the air induced him to stop and consider his situation.

We all jumped out, and I immediately put the bike back where it was supposed to be, because I am pretty sure I would have ridden the beef for swiping the bike. Dick would have rolled over on me to take the rap.

Needless to say, it caused a bit of an uproar!

Folks were rubbernecking around, as the Dicks scrambled to find a way to turn the giant gasoline spray off. Tony and I backed off, wondering if we should just start hitchhiking and abandon the "adults" to their fate.

The store guy showed up pretty quick, and opened the store to hit the shut-off switch staunching the flow of the spurting potential fireball.

The truck was unscathed.

The gas pump was 15 feet away, and crushed pretty good, with bits of metal and broken glass strewn about. There was a 30-foot circle of gasoline soaking the ground that could have burned like a napalm strike, and the Dicks were having an argument about Dirty Dick's driving abilities.

The big kahuna of the lodge showed up and approached the Dicks. To be sure, the guy was somewhat apprehensive. Dirty Dick said to him, "What are you going to do about my truck?"

"Your truck?" he said. "What about the gas pump?"

"Fuck that gas pump! Tell Rockefeller to send me a bill!"

The lodge guy says, "You have been drinking."

"Yes," says Dirty Dick, "and you kicked us out!"

I did not recall getting kicked out myself. In for a penny, in for a pound, I guess.

That is when the Park Ranger showed up.

He was not a very big fellow, and the Smoky Bear hat must have been too big because he kept adjusting it. This was long before Park Rangers looked like SWAT team members and were packing heat. He was packing a big flashlight, and when he took it out Dick Robbins said, "Put that back, before I shove it up your ass!"

The guy put it back.

Dirty Dick was arguing with the lodge manager, who finally threw his arms up in the air and said, "OK, OK! But will you leave in the morning!?"

In frustration, the guy had given Dirty Dick a cabin in the back, if we would just go away and leave in the morning. Early!

We pulled the truck around back, and we went to a pretty nice little cabin. They would not give the Dicks any more whiskey, so they conked out pretty quick. Tony and I sat up and split my hostess cherry pie that was as hard as a whore's heart, and we played cards.

The next day, we got up early because we were hungry and went and got the Datsun station wagon. It still had the batteries and tires, so off we went to Aberdeen,

24 hours after we left

I did not tell my mom for years. 45 years as it turns out because I just talked to her today and told her about what I was writing. She said, "Huh, I haven't heard that one before."

GETTING TO ALASKA
AS A KID

I recall my summer of '73 some, and would have been 13, nearly 14, when Dick was sentenced to Alaska—which, in those days, meant if you had a warrant out in the Lower 48, and were in the tramp logging game, you ran away to Alaska and worked in logging camps.

Would have been early July, and he and his new young wife and her daughter had landed in Ketchikan, located on the southern part of the Panhandle. And back in those days—before the airport was built on the island across from town, where one takes a little ferry to, these days—you had to fly into the airport in Juneau, then take a plane that lands on water back to Ketchikan.

Dick had gotten a job in Thorne Bay. Driving truck, if memory serves—I cannot imagine he would have been in the brush.

Steve Esterby was probably setting chokers there at the time, and Dick had gotten his small new family all set up at the luxurious accommodations above the Foc'sle Bar—a notorious bar and logger roughhouse that rented out small rooms upstairs with a shared kitchen and bathroom, and small TV room that looked out over the Tongass Narrows.

We would have been at the beginning of the family carving game in Humptulips, at that time, because Mike and Joy had just relocated from France with an infant Noelle.

At any rate, it was decided that I would spend some time with Daddy that summer, and he sent a ticket for me to travel north for some paternal bonding.

Judy wasn't all that enthusiastic, but relented because she had a pretty full plate running the new family carving compound, and one less mouth to feed for a couple of months wouldn't hurt, I suppose.

I was all fired up to go on an adventure, and maybe start having my own stories.

It worked—I got a story.

On the morning of my departure, Mike was to take me to the airport at SeaTac and I was to fly to Juneau and then to Ketchikan. Seemed simple enough.

I don't recall if I had my ticket on me, or had to go to the counter and get it.

We went by his friend Edna Fox's ("Foxy"—she was so cool) place in Olympia for a visit and were not too far from the airport. Then we went to some breakfast place, and, when we were there, he had me get him some cigarettes out of a vending machine.

When I hit the change return, it spat out a bunch of

quarters, so I hit it again, and more came out! Kept playing, 'till I got about five dollars.

We got to the airport, and Mike dropped me off at
the curb and said, "Have a nice flight." He had flown all
over the world at that point, and maybe assumed it was
easy peasy. Plus it was two dollars to park.

I was on the curb with my $20 bill and a pocket full
of change, looking every bit the country bumpkin that I
was, when up dances a Hare Krishna disciple with some
bright eyes and a topknot of sorts.

He started quizzing me on life, and after confusing
the shit out of me he offered up a book to open my eyes
and said it was only a dollar.

Being as I enjoyed reading, and was about to embark
on a flight, I said, "Sure. I'll spend a dollar on a book."

So I ponied up my $20 bill, expecting some change,
and he said "Be right back," and danced back into the
crowd. Never saw any change, and the book was incom-
prehensible gibberish. . . . The learning curve is steep for
country bumpkins, and, even though I did not know it
at the time, my informal education had just begun, and
caution became something that I was to begin exercising
a little better!

This is before I even went into the airport wearing
my upside-down sweatshirt with the sleeves tied into a
knot full of my stuff, and I found the way that led to the
gate where I was to depart from.

I noticed the metal detectors one walked through to

get to the correct gate, and, while I did not have any weaponry, I did have my clamshell eyeglass case. It was made of some kind of metal, and I had it stuffed full of pre-rolled joints . . . and beings as I had just bought a $20 book that taught me to be more cautious, I went in the restroom and transferred all those joints to some plastic wrap and into the super-safe smuggling location of my sock.

Bigger than shit, the eyeglass case made it beep! Trust your gut, folks; it's seldom wrong.

Caught the plane, and it was a couple-hour flight to Juneau. It landed in that beautiful town and I was to wait a few hours to catch the floatplane back to Ketchikan, so I wandered around the airport. And since I had luckily won some money on the cigarette slot machine, I could stave off hunger some with vending machines.

At any rate, being a novice to traveling on my own— and having possibly sampled some of my sock baggage —I missed the plane back to Ketchikan and called Dick up. He got ahold of Alaska Airlines and chewed on their ass for losing his poor little thirteen-year-old son in their airport!

I just stayed by the phone (all pay phones in those days) and waited for a while. I called back after a bit, and Dick said, "Go to the ticket counter. They've been looking for you, and will take care of it."

Worked my way over to the tickets counter, and announced, "Did my dad get ahold of you guys about me? I missed my flight to Ketchikan."

They all looked up at me in disbelief, and they were standing up themselves, and said, "You are thirteen!? We have been looking all over for you!"

At the time, I was about six foot tall and weighed about 180, but the way Dick described me was as a poor little thirteen-year-old lost in the maze!

Alaska Airlines put me up at the Baranof Downtown and supplied dinner. I had two steak and lobster dinners and tried for a beer but she just laughed and said no.

Had to hitchhike into town and back to the airport. Made the flight to Ketchikan, and the summer living over the top of the Foc'sle Bar was a source of many more stories that will leak out at some point.

SWATS AND SOTH

Pretty much everything that dribbles out of my head is a recollection of mine, or stories told to me by others in my life. Some funny, some thoughtful, some kind of sad or tragic, but usually with a twist of humor.

But along the path, the dragons do come to call, from time to time. These experiences—our own, or others—we may take as lessons, albeit hard lessons, at times. But the mark or scar is made and, hidden or visible, it's there. Let the lesson be wisdom or knowledge; or both.

Getting all weepy and windy here, but like the great American philosopher Jimmy Buffet says, "We are just a bunch of Monkeys with PhDs."

This tale is from grade school and another time and age. It was for sure in the wild western Olympics of Washington State, in the late 1960s, where the Lake Quinault School was/is located—in Amanda Park on Highway 101, in the northern part of Grays Harbor.

Rough place, what with the waning age of the "Golden Days of Logging." Big trees and tough loggers were a dime a dozen.

It was at this school in what I believe was 1968 or 69–fourth grade for me. My smart mouth earned me some "swats" from Mr. Soth—the vice principal, if memory serves. He always seemed to have a couple of miscreants lined up in the hallway at lunchtime for swats with his cricket bat-like paddle.

"Bend over and grab your ankles," and you could hear the whack if you were outside listening for it, or just walking by at the moment when the wooden bat made contact with a young boy's buttocks. He must have liked doing it because it seemed he always had a few customers.

This school is so small, it was on NPR once as the modern-day equivalent of a one-room schoolhouse, with first through twelfth grades all in the same one-story school building. So our rate of troublemakers was extraordinarily high!

When I mentioned that I was a candidate for swats from Mr. Soth to Dick and Judy, it was at a time when they were getting ready for a divorce. And smart-mouth kids getting some comeuppance from the school over-lords wasn't on the radar, as they had less than reason-able debates on each other's faults to think about.

But, to give the devil his due, Dick said, "Oh yeah? We will see about that," as I went to bed with my last supper in my belly. . . .

The next day, as I awaited the appointed hour in our

fourth grade classroom, there was a bit of a commotion down the hall where the teachers' lounge was. It was their sanctuary, where they could smoke cigarettes, swill coffee, and complain about troublesome students of which it seemed there was no shortage.

Dick was in the teachers' lounge, informing Mr. Soth that, "Whatever you do to my kid, I'll do to you, you big, fat, motherfucker!"

No Swats for me . . . instead I had to copy a page out of a dictionary! Swats were looking good now.

It has recently occurred to me that Dirty Dick Backus, and his public humiliation of Mr. Soth, might of had some influence on the rest of this story.

The memory dredge doesn't always bring up the pleasant stuff, but up she comes: We had a fellow fourth grader who had a sister in the third or second grade, and they had a single mom who tended bar down in Amanda Park, where they lived.

At times, young Jim would slip off to home at lunchtime, but it was a closed campus and it was not allowed, even to hungry fourth graders. And with the high hill of age to look back with, and having been a perpetually hungry kid myself, it is easy to figure out: He was hungry!

And for this high crime, he was to be punished, because schools had not clued in on the simple formula that kids do better if they ain't hungry!

Seems simple nowadays, but we are talking about

the olden days here.

At any rate, Mr. Soth figured to make a fine example of demonstrating his authority over this flock of trouble-makers, as young Jim kept defying his jowl-jiggling commands to cease going home at lunchtime and stay on school grounds.

It is my thought that because he knew (it was a small community) that young Jim did not have a logger dad—who would show up and beat him up—he decided that the punishment would be to march this young fellow into each classroom from first to sixth grades and give him three whacks in each classroom. It would be a pub-licly humiliating demonstration of the vice principal's absolute authority over his flock of troublemakers, and, as mentioned earlier, there were many. . . .

You could hear it coming up the hallway, room by room—a lot of wailing and door-slamming—and, by the time they got to the fourth grade classroom, Jim was a mess. He was crying, and squirming around pretty good, but Fat Freddie had a pretty good hold on him by the back of the neck.

His t-shirt was torn by then, and I've got to give Jim some credit for being a handful, but it would throw Mr. Soth's aim off, some. And a lot of the swats missed the buttocks, and landed anywhere from his mid-back, to his knees. But Soth was in a froth by then, all red-faced and determined to see it through.

When this awful spectacle had gone through his sister's classroom, she bolted out the door and ran down and told her mom. So, by the time Soth got into the fifth grade classroom, Jim's mom showed up with talons extended, and proved that the women in logger country were as tough and fearless as any man out there.

She lit into him like a mamma grizzly bear protecting a cub.

He had scratch marks on his rotund face for a while, and I believe he went to jail, where, perhaps, he was asked to bend over and grab his ankles.

Needless to say, "swats" became a thing of the past, in that small school, and for those that think we need to return to that sort of thing, please reread this. . . .

LYLE GETS RID
OF THE PUPPIES

One never knows what the memory dredge churns up, and in talking with my sister Lynn a while back, we glanced across a recollection she had of a day in the neighborhood of our childhood in the little burg of Humptulips, in western Washington, back in the early 1970s.

It would be safe to say that in those days the whole "spay and neuter your pets" program was in its infancy. And the way in which unwanted puppies and kittens were disposed of was a somewhat brutal affair, though it was an accepted practice, and, in hindsight, it is a little scary that some enjoyed the work!

At any rate, my mom's dear friend Kay lived down off Kirkpatrick Road, and her neighbor's dog had some pups that Lyle was supposed to have dispatched soon after their arrival. But he procrastinated some, and, as mentioned in an earlier tale, you didn't need a dog in Humptulips in those days—you just needed a sack of dog food.

Many procrastinated on this task, which certainly had some unpleasantness that came with it, and Kay's neighbor's puppies had started getting around pretty good. Mable had been on Lyle's ass to do something about it, but he had not.

One afternoon, when Lyle rolled in with his Ford pickup truck, the pups had gotten into the garbage and had it scattered all over hell's half acre.

Mable was pissed and lit into him as soon as he parked the truck. He called the dents and scratches in his pick-up truck "whiskey Bumps," of which there were more than a few, and he may have been sampling firewater at the time.

Lynn, and I am sure Debbie, were outside playing. At the time they must have been ten or eleven when Lyle rolled in and the ruckus started up next door. Like many small communities, a good domestic ruckus was the entertainment channel at the time, and this was shaping up to be a good one, as Lyle and Mable started screaming at each other about the dogs, and the garbage, how he fucked up, and just what in the hell do we do about it now!?

Lynn says that he threw his arms up in the air, went in the house, came back out with his trusty 300 Savage semi-automatic, and proceed to dispose of the puppies/half-grown dogs. He was a good shot, as mentioned in another tale of mine when he was gathering government Beef.

Kay gathered up the kids quick as a wink into her house, and Lynn said he got every puppy—all nine of them—and then shot the cat off the neighbor's roof, where it had sought refuge!

Just another day in the neighborhood I suppose, and it could explain Lynn's compulsion to save every living thing that comes across her path. No shit, she could fill an ark with her saves over the years, from emus, to chickens, to horses and pigs, to pretty much anything that needs saving if she is nearby.

Just a couple years back, Princess NoNo told me of a time when she and Lynn were at a busy intersection, just off the freeway in Idaho, when she spotted a little bird in a busy four-way intersection.

She stopped her truck and got out, dodging semis and commuters, to shepherd that little bird off the road. Nanette was scared for her the whole time, but Lynn just bailed in and did it.

I love my little sister—she is one of the toughest people I know. One of the most caring, as well.

ESCAPE FROM FAIRBANKS

I often reflect upon the adventures with Dirty Dick Backus, and a chuckle will often bubble up from some of the shit he pulled, and in most cases got away with (most cases.) I suppose Lee Marvin could have captured his character, like a rascal out of *Paint Your Wagon* or *Cat Ballou.*

At any rate, like a lot of logger types that ran off to Alaska in the 1970s, he ended up latching onto the golden goose known as the "Alaskan Pipeline," and he extracted many a dollar from that deep-pocketed project for over a decade. Many of the tales and exploits, told over adult beverages with his contemporaries, were a source of wonder at all they got away with!

Like many tramp logger types that hit the big money on the "Slope," he spent it mostly on liquor and whores, with some dribbling back to owed child support after Judy sicced the government on him for his squandering ways. . . . And squander he did!

He once sent a bumper sticker that said "Please, God, grant us another pipeline; we promise to not piss this one away."

In 1982, when Princess NoNo and I were just beginning our mating rituals, Ki was having a big Halloween
party that Nanette was going to be at . . . and we were
not "official," as of yet, but I was smitten somewhat, and
wanted to go to the party.

About a week or so before the party, Dirty Dick
Backus calls up from Fairbanks and says he'd just done
12 weeks on the slope and wants to get a Cadillac and
drive to Mexico. "So hop a plane and get up here so we
can make the journey!"

This was a bit of a dilemma for me because I wanted
to hit the party, but adventures with Richard were always interesting, and I hatched a plan to get up there
and tie the return trip into a stop back on the Island for
a few days, so I could make it to the party.

The best-laid plans of mice and men; what could go
wrong!?

He sent a ticket, and I made the plane. As I recall,
there was still smoking on planes then, and I made it to
Fairbanks just fine and began my babysitting of Dirty
Dick Backus—which could be exhausting, but I was of
the mind that we would buy a car and head out before
winter was gripping that land too hard.

Seemed easy enough, but Richard had an active so-
cial scene in Fairbanks and was a heavy contributor
to many bars and lounges. He helped them with their
mortgage payments, often very generously, and keeping

up with his daily activities—which consisted of visiting these establishments on a well-regulated routine from morning to evening—was a chore. But I was a bit of a pest on the whole, "Let's get a car and get going!" and we finally settled on a VW Bug that some folks had just driven up from Florida. So that part was done, but Dick kinda viewed it as saving money on cabs, as I drove him around to his watering holes and as he paid me off with "shut up money." I stashed it every time and started a rat hole that ended up saving my ass.

We stayed at his stepsister's place while in that town, where he had a pretty good setup, and she was a very nice, very patient lady about her unruly stepsibling.

Each day consisted of driving him to a bar, and him getting irritated with me for nagging about leaving. He had over $20,000 in uncashed paychecks in his brief-case, at his sister's, but was burning through it at an alarming rate, so separating him from that town and aiming him south was becoming somewhat more urgent!

After a few days of the lounge tour, where he seemed to know everyone or knew someone they knew, my nagging began to wear on him. I would go to the bathroom, and when I came back out he would have disappeared, caught a cab, and gone to another bar.

He would always get a big grin when I found him, and the games continued until I threatened to just take off without him. After that, he would chuckle and then the hide-and-seek would continue.

He would give me money as we went along, but my liver in no way could compete with his battle-hardened one, and I stashed my loot and plotted my escape. Soon, my date of departure became critical, to make it from Fairbanks, Alaska, to Whidbey Island, in Washington State, and the party where Princess NoNo was to be in attendance.

So, when I left, it was the last week of October and my plan was to drive to Haines, Alaska, and take the ferry to Prince Rupert, British Columbia, then drive down through Hope and get back to the Island in time for the party.

Best-laid plans of mice and men.

I headed out, and there did not seem to be a button for the heater. I just wore the big insulated coveralls that Dick had gotten me and kept a roll of paper towels handy to wipe a little porthole to see out of. Driving, I listened to the only tape I had . . . which had happened to be in the car when we got it, and it was Helen Reddy and her "I am Woman, Hear Me Roar." Radio reception being what it was in the far north, I could sing it backwards by the time I got to Hope where the radio reception was good.

As I left Fairbanks, I must have drove a hundred miles or better when my hand was feeling around on its own and found some little levers between the seats. So, I just pulled up on them to see what happened, and was flooded with heat!

Apparently, the heat button was not on the dash-board in VWs, but a lever between the seats. This was welcome news, and on I drove, heading to Chilkoot Pass right out of a Robert Service poem. And as I was travel-ing along, to that storied pass, I noticed that the reflec-tors alongside the road were really tall and thought it odd, until it dawned on me that the snow got that deep at some point!

Very motivating that was, and I longed to see saltwa-ter where dying in a snowbank was less likely. As I cau-tiously descended down into Haines, Alaska, I had the good fortune to witness thousands of bald eagles feeding on salmon in the rivers and deltas. It was magnificent, and when I first noticed them, they were in trees . . . I counted over 50 in a mile, then came to an area where one could see the rivers, and they were thick as crows in a dumpster.

Got a ticket to Prince Rupert, and stayed the night so as to leave very early. I did a little walkabout in that little town and bought a pair of Carhartt pants and had no experience with that particular workwear at that time. Damn, they were good pants! Wore 'em till they rotted off me, and then burned them ceremoniously. Been a Carhartt fan ever since.

Ferry stopped in Ketchikan for a few hours, and I went to a house that Dick owned but rented out, except for a little studio upstairs where he had a bunk and kitchen. There I pilfered some goods, like a pistol and tools (advice from Judy; "back support" she called it,) and then headed off to northern B.C.

I rolled off the boat on a fine sunny morning, heading to Prince George so as to turn south towards civilization, and the big party where Princess NoNo would be with her rowdy, and often scary, softball teammates. They were a funny, strong bunch of gals, and since I had been listening to Helen Reddy belting out "I am Woman" for a thousand miles, I was already a little intimidated!

I soldiered on, and drove throughout the day and night, and, as I recall, the radio seemed to work by the time I got to Hope, well past midnight. I gave Helen Reddy a well-deserved break, and on the radio they were talking about a movie that was being filmed in that town called *First Blood*, based on a book I had read. I was of the thought that there would be a lot of bloodshed in the movie, and I was right. It became Judy's favorite Christmas movie and she would play the jailbreak scene over and over!

I crossed the border at Sumas, and that put me at about three hours from my destination. I had been jacked on coffee for about 30 hours, at that point, but wanted to get back to the comfortable bosom of South Whidbey.

I made it to my mom's place at about ten o'clock in the morning and gave her $500 of my rat hole money from her rotten ex-husband. We both had a chuckle at how hard it was to collect back child support.

I made it to the big Halloween party, and Princess NoNo was radiant as I spewed out my long tale of seas crossed and mountains overcome to get to the fair princess!

Her brother Greg was dumbfounded that his sister fell for a chainsaw carver.

Dick still did not believe I had left him and thought I was avoiding him until he sobered up. He showed up at the SeaTac Airport, flat broke and needing a ride to Dick Robbins' (of the Kalaoch gas pump story,) house to borrow some money and a truck.

He burned through that $20,000 in two months in Fairbanks, then flew south to stay with his mom until the slope opened up some, and he could head north to repeat what was becoming a yearly routine.

MARVIN CRUM GETS SHOT

Marvin was the son of Roger Crum, who became friends with Dick Backus sometime in the 1950s while logging the "Redweeds" in Orick, California, when they both stayed at a boardinghouse. It was still there, the last time I went through that small town in Northern California, and that town boasts the most chainsaw carving shops per square inch these days than anywhere else.

Dirty Dick and his good friend Steve Trojen—who was an Armenian but was known in the timber tramp loop as the "One-Eyed Wap"—were staying at the boardinghouse, and Dick and the Wap were using quite a lot of foul language at the dinner table. Roger asked them to clean their language up, or perhaps he would shut their mouths for them.

Being as Roger was bigger, tougher, in his prime, and so very capable of fulfilling his promise to the young tramps, they complied with so many "please and thank yous," that it was nearly as irritating to Roger. He had to chuckle, and he and Dick became friends from then on, until Roger kicked the bucket a decade later in

Aberdeen.

Bumped a memory to the surface just now, and it would have to be one of my earliest memories regarding a chainsaw, wouldn't it? It involved Roger and was before I was in School, so about 1965, I reckon. Before Boaz was in the picture. Roger stopped by, looking for Dick, and had been at the "Wirta," a notorious tramp logger bar in Aberdeen that was just a few blocks away from where we lived at the time.

Roger was a timber feller who was good at it, and had just bought a chainsaw and was sitting at the kitchen table telling Judy all about it, as I watched and listened, holding my Siamese cat. Since Roger was all boozed up, he decided to show Judy his new saw, because he was proud of it, and in those days a saw like that was an investment for a timber tramp.

He came back inside with the saw, and it had no bar in it, but was a sizable piece of equipment to a four-year-old. Judy was not carving at the time, but knew all about chainsaws, so knew how important it was to him for what he had to do with it, and that he was really proud of it. He said, "Starts right up on the first pull! You wanna hear it roar?"

She said, "NO!" as he pulled the starter rope, and, bigger than shit, it blasted to life in that small kitchen like a grenade!

That Siamese cat went up my face and down my back at full speed, laying me open like a good lashing with a cat o' nine tails, and Roger left shortly thereafter. . . .

Now, where was I. . . .

Judy and Dick knew *Marvin* Crum since he was 17, and years later he became a timber feller in the tramp logger world, and a good one in his own right.

He was working in southeastern Alaska by then, must have been 1970-71, or so, and the bears were has-sling the fellers. Marvin told of walking around a tree and coming face-to-face with a big bear sitting on its haunches eating Marvin's lunch, and when it saw Marvin it started growling and slapping its jaws together. Marvin said it was like two giant dinner platters coming together with slobber spraying ten feet.

Marvin beat a hasty retreat, and the boss handled the problem by issuing all the fellers .45 magnums. And back into the woods they went to log them big trees, and it was not long before Marvin was back in the bunkhouse at the end of the day. He dropped his draw-ers a little fast, and that big pistol was still in its holster, but apparently not on safety, because when it hit the deck it went off and shot a big hole right through his leg. He said it made him do a complete somersault!

They shipped him off to Ketchikan, Alaska, and when the word got out that Marvin was in the hospi-tal and needed blood, the timber tramps heeded the call and the bars emptied out as they climbed the hill to help Marvin!

As Marvin told it, so many drunks showed up to give blood that he got a little buzz on. But, unfortunately, he got Hepatitis C out of the deal, and it came back to haunt him decades later.

He lamented that if he would have shot himself a day later, the law would have changed, and the settlement would have been double. But it took effect the day after his incident, and as Dirty Dick Backus often said, "That's the way she goes. First your money, then your clothes."

Marvin took his money and went back to Puget Sound, and bought a sailboat. He lived in that boat and his van the rest of his life, which was as eventful as one might imagine it could be, now that he sailed the not-so-high seas of the Salish Sea, and earned his moniker of Captain Blood!

Marvin was a timber tramp, and a close friend of the McBackus clan for many, many years.

MARVIN AND LOOSE BARK

Many a Marvin Crum story was mentioned in casual conversation around a big table, or campfire, and Marvin had a few that were about avoiding sudden death. There were many of these stories from these guys who existed in an occupation where sudden, tragic death was not uncommon. The quick thinkers were often around later, to recount the tale, or, as was often the case, to recount the demise of the not-so-quick thinkers.

Once again, this took place in Southeastern, Alaska in the 1960s, and a young Marvin Crum was working in a logging camp located out of Ketchikan. I'm unsure where, but they were working and bringing the logs to the saltwater, in this little bay, to make a raft for the tugs to tow to the mills.

As the rafts grew, it required the loggers to run around on the rafts and tuck all the logs in proper, and chain them together, so they would not come apart while under tow. There were hard dangers and it was equally hard, physical work, in which they ran around with poles and peaveys, adjusting logs until everything was as good as could be for the tow.

Everything moved around Southeastern, Alaska by water, between those rugged, beautiful islands and the opening of the Tongass Forest, in the early 1960s. It was not long after Alaska became a state, and the tramp loggers flocked there like migrating timber beasts, and Marvin would have been in the thick of it, in those days.

It would be fair to say that the log rolling competitions we see at fairs and exhibitions are a direct descendant of this tricky dance, in which balance and strength are married together to do a tough job and avoid dying. As anyone who has tried standing on a log in the water knows, it ain't easy. And when we watch the log rolling at a fair, it is my thought that most folks watching haven't a clue how hard it is!

But if you fall off the log at the fair, you can bounce up out of a few feet of water and do it again. And sometimes it's even heated water! Our log show here on Whidbey Island has a marvel of engineering by Albert Gabelein, that is a wood-fired heater that heats the water . . . but not much, and you can't tell, but I admire his trying.

At any rate, Marvin told of an early fall morning where he was eager to do the rafting, and, in the youthful exuberance, had kind of run ahead of the rest of the crew, to the log raft. He was dressed for a cold morning in the wet southeast of Alaska, with long johns, heavy pants, hickory shirt, rain gear, tin hat, and calk boots

(those are heavy work boots with spikes on the bottoms, used for traction while scampering about on log piles—whether in the brush or on a log raft.)

This raft was mostly made up of Sitka spruce, with some cedar as well. As anyone familiar with these trees knows, the bark on a western red cedar is long and stringy, and on the big, old growth that they were logging it can be pretty thick, as well. So, he was aware that the calk boots could tear out of the surface of a cedar because it was spongy, and the traction could be tricky.

These logs could be, on average, four to six feet across, and were like whales at rest. Young Marvin went running across the raft, and, as he got to the edge, he was on a big Sitka spruce. The bark was different on spruce, with a lot more traction because of the way it grows, and is thinner too, so the calk boots gripped it just fine.

If a tree is cut in the winter the bark is tight to the tree, and you would need a draw knife to peel it, but, if cut in the spring when the sap is running, the bark is loose, because the tree is waking up from winter and sending lots of good tree juice up the trunk. That way, there is a good separation of tree and bark.

As Marvin recalled, he skidded to a stop on this big spruce log, and a chunk of bark the size of a throw rug where his calk boots dug in, came loose and dumped him straight away into the water.

This little bay was about fifteen feet deep at high

tide . . . and it was high tide.

He said, as he went down, he was looking up and watching bubbles. He was thinking fast, and knew in a heartbeat he would never swim back up with all his gear on, especially with those big, heavy calk boots acting like little anchors. They were taking him down for a crab feed, except it would be the crabs doing the feasting!

He knew that the bay bottom was pretty much gravel, so he bent his knees, and when he hit bottom he kicked straight back up through his bubbles, and made it to the surface long enough to get his arm on a log. He grabbed a bit of a knot and yelled as loud as the air left in him would allow!

The rest of the crew was just approaching the raft and heard the commotion, so they ran out and drug his ass out of the water.

They were unsympathetic to his wet clothes, and since they were there to do a job, that's what they did. Marvin said he was a little more careful, but finished the day in wet clothes.

Just another day at the office. . . .

THE BIG REWARD

I've been on a bit of a childhood memory kick, remembering all the tramp logger culture that I was raised in, there on the wild Olympic Peninsula and Southeastern Alaska, at the tail-end of the old growth logging era. I heard many a story, as I sat in the background of many of these creatures who inhabited the land, and were also constant visitors at our home, wherever we lived.

There were many of these fellows, from young to old, and, to a kid, they were all whiskey-drinking, Copenhagen-chewing warriors that did battle with giants. I was endlessly fascinated, and all ears, and I put down what I recall, as best I can, because few are left to ask questions. So, details are lost in the telling.

My dad, Dick Backus, was firmly entrenched in this tramp logging culture and was a creative fellow. He was logging in the Eureka, California area, sometime in the early/mid-1950s, and he had a dog. Don't know if I ever knew the name of this dog, since this was years before I came along and ruined his life! This dog was his best friend, and was a handsome animal as I understand it—

traveled everywhere with him in his logging truck, as Dirty Dick Backus hauled loads of big redwood around that rugged country.

He told a story once of hauling a load during a rainstorm—which, in Northern California, can be an astounding amount of water, capable of raising the rivers and washing out ten, or fifteen, foot diameter redwood trees right on out to the Pacific Ocean. If you've ever been on those beaches in Northern California, and seen a tree like that on the beach, remember that it started out in the mountains!

I've even heard stories of these giant logs that are waterlogged to the point of sinking, and that fishing boats have run afoul of them with their nets and been taken down. I don't know if it is true, but it would seem to be within the realm of possibility.

It was the end of the day, and Dick was hauling the last load of the day. If memory serves, it was the Klamath River, and he was contemplating crossing a bridge that was a shortcut to the mill. Being the end of the day, he was reluctant to drive to the main highway, because it took another 45 minutes, and he and his good buddy—the fine, boxer dog—wanted to get to dinner.

As he sat in the truck, with the downpour making the river about level with the backroad bridge, he was thinking that maybe he had better take the long way, and just back up and turn around. As he watched the raging river, a giant redwood tree rootball came barreling down the river and just took that bridge out!

I exclaimed, "Holy shit! You could've been killed!" and he said, "Yeah, I'm lucky like that."

He and his dog delivered the load to the mill and went to dinner, and he took his dog in the restaurant with him and ordered two steak dinners. When he got the dinners, he gave one to the dog and told the waitress that when he ate beans, his dog ate beans, so when he eats steak, his dog eats steak.

At some point, his dog came up missing and he was of the mind someone stole him. But, just in case, he put an ad in the paper saying that he was looking for his dog, and offered a "BIG REWARD." By God, someone showed up with the dog the next day and was eager to get his big reward.

Dick rolled out a new log truck tire and said, "Here ya go. . . . It's big. . . ."

WORKBENCH TROUBLES

Back in my childhood, the tramp logger culture was all around me, and I listened to those wild creatures laugh, talk, and argue about everything from the camps they worked in, to the equipment they used. They were, for the most part, a hard-drinking, tough crew that were always in transition, it seemed, either heading from or going to some logging job.

In those days, anyone that hitchhiked up or down Highway 101 with a pair of cork boots over their shoulder, could be working by noon, if they were on the road in the morning, anywhere from Northern California to the top of the Olympic Peninsula.

When Alaska became a state in 1959, and they opened up the Tongass Forest in Southeastern Alaska, logging became a much bigger deal up there, and the tramp loggers began to migrate there in bigger numbers. It was not uncommon to have the timber beasts migrate from Northern California to Alaska, and, as a kid, I encountered many who traveled this path as they moved around. It was transitory work by its very nature—cut the trees down, and move on.

Getting fired or quitting, for whatever reason, was normal, and finding work was easy if you wanted to work.

Dirty Dick Backus was banished to Alaska in the early 1970s and ended up in Ketchikan, where he took up residence above the Foc'sle Bar—a notorious bar in that wild town. It was said that more loggers were hired out of that bar than the Employment Security office. They had a chalkboard in that bar with jobs being offered, and a tramp logger just had to show up and pick. One time, some smart ass put on the board that they were running a night shift at some camp and the logger needed to supply his own black ox gloves.

The summer I turned 14, I was sent off to stay with Dirty Dick Backus for the summer. It would have been 1973, and I was up there for a couple months until school started back in Humptulips, in the fall.

My stepmom (I don't actually know if they actually got married) was a bartender downstairs at the Foc'sle, and never let it be said that Dirty Dick Backus ever let a woman miss a shift! She would work the late shift, and, in Alaska, in those days the Foc'sle Bar closed at 5:00 A.M. and then opened back up at 6:00 A.M.!

All the drunks would go outside for an hour, to drink on the sidewalk and smoke cigarettes, waiting for the door to open back up.

I would go down at about 5:00, and help her stock

beer and all the other stuff that needed to be packed and stacked, as she swept the floor and restocked.

The doors would open back up, and in they would come. So I would enjoy my breakfast of those ham sandwiches you baked in those little ovens before microwaves were in the picture, and drink coke with ice, as those hard-drinking wild men—and a few ladies—would swarm back in and pick up where they left off an hour prior.

I turned 14 that July and was a big lad, so I could fit on a bar stool, and it was legal for kids to be in a bar up there, if with a parent, and my stepmom was the bartender. It would be safe to say that this was long before Betty Ford got things going with rehabs and alcohol counseling, and some of these guys would booze themselves into oblivion, and fall right off the bar stool onto the less-than-pristine floor—that was filthy as a rule. They would be passed out right where they fell, next to their stool, head on the footrail.

I suppose these days they would call an ambulance and a couple counselors, but, in those days on the wild frontier, the bartender would just take their drink off the bar and set it down behind the bar. After a while, a couple hands would appear on the edge of the bar, the over-served logger would climb back on his stool, and the bartender would set their drinks back in front of them.

When you are a kid, whatever is going on in your life is the only normal that you have to compare things to, so sitting with drunken loggers telling stories was normal for me. And, often, I would be the recipient of tales. Since I was a kid with no stories of my own, I kept my mouth shut and soaked it up.

Kinda windy on the backstory, but just laying out a timeline of sorts and where my head was at the time. I had no idea how this would affect my life down the road, being exposed to those independent operators, who did not care if school was kept or not.

I was there one fine, rainy morning, in the company of a bar full of drunken loggers, a few fishermen, Indians, and maybe an occasional brave hippie. Many that were in there were friends of Dirty Dick, who I had known my whole life, and I had no friends my own age at all but was on the edge of this circle of fellows. I just listened, for the most part. I had nothing to offer but an ear, in many cases.

I was seated next to a logger from Forks, Washington, who was new in town, and I had mentioned that I went to the Lake Quinault school, thus putting our conversation to where he worked in Forks for some gypo logger. I believe, because I was such a large lad (6' and 180lbs at 14), that those guys thought I was a young want-to-be, but I had just gotten out of the eighth grade.

At any rate, this logger told me that he worked for old so-and-so and that this guy was a screamer and was always yelling at his help. This guy was a mechanic in the shop, where the gypo logger in charge had a nice setup, with all the good tools, and a big, long stainless steel workbench that he was very proud of. But, he was, according to the logger, an insufferable prick with all the screaming and yelling.

And, in the time-honored tradition of quitting a job that you did not like, he did just that and headed for Alaska, for a new job—which, as mentioned earlier, was not difficult at all. Pretty much just had to show up ready to work.

This logger claimed to be a pretty good mechanic and welder, and he said the screamer in Forks did have a lot of good tools, and that wonderful, long stainless steel workbench that was a pleasure to work on. So, after he got his ticket north and was about to depart, in a last act of defiance he welded the screamer's entire socket and wrench set to that big, beautiful workbench!

It is my thought that, in many ways, I am trying to replicate my chainsaw carving community in the mold of the tramp loggers, with many of the characteristics being somewhat similar in their own ways. What with the rugged independence, and the ability to go nearly anywhere to work, and then move on as the fancy strikes. It would also be fair to say booze can play a part, but it should be something to outgrow. (Should be.)

MARVIN GETS A TICKET

It is no secret that I was raised in an environment that was not necessarily baseball, apple pie, and church on Sunday . . . but it was character-building, for sure. And if one had a rough go of it as a kid, my advice would be to read more books and reach into oneself for direction.

Just saying.

It would be fair to say that chainsaw carving is really good therapy, and my guess is that lots of carvers would agree. So channel what's in ya, and be nice.

At any rate, I am trying to write a story a day for a few days, to teach myself a little discipline, which is hard for me, at times. Discipline is one of the hardest things to master about working for yourself, so, once it's light outside, I have a hard time staying indoors—because, if one is to sell woodcarvings, one must make them.

And when one has had a dragon eat everything up, and forced you to start from scratch, it takes a minute to get back up to speed. I lost better than a month on my midwinter musings, so I'm getting jacked on coffee and attempting to catch up with what wants out of my head.

One of the tramp loggers that was consistent in my life until he died, was Marvin Crum, and one of the stories concerning him was repeated many times—and I even heard it from him. Of course, it concerns a drunk logger or two, and a creative solution to a vexing problem.

It would have been the late 1960s, or thereabouts, and Marvin was working in Alaska at a logging camp sometime before he shot himself in the leg, as told in an earlier tale. He had gone to Ketchikan for the weekend, and ended up at the infamous Foc'sle Bar, as many did, and was getting himself a skin full, as he put it.

He had passed out in the problem solvers' corner. This was the corner of the bar where the elders sat and drank, and came up with solutions to problems, and some were rather comical, depending on your view.

A fellow problem solver entered the bar and sat in the corner, and pronounced that he had been drinking, and, on the drive to the bar, had sideswiped a parked car. He was of the mind the cops would be along shortly, and he just couldn't get another drunk driving ticket and was thinking he had better catch a plane south, to avoid dealing with it.

It was his lucky day, because he had seated himself with a group of excellent solution providers!

They quickly came to the conclusion that since the young Marvin Crum had no tickets, and was peacefully slumbering away in the corner, he was not busy at the moment. So, the whole crew carried the unconscious Marvin out and put him in the car. Problem solved!

They wandered back to the corner to save the world.

Marvin said he woke up in jail, but the crew had bail money ready and he was back at the Foc'sle Bar in good time.

WALLY LOWERS A BODY

Growing up in logging country as a youngster, stories and tales were told and retold as I lurked in the background with big ears. Those unvarnished logger types told of things that went wrong, and they could be very funny, as they tended to tell them with dark humor. In hindsight, that was a coping device for many of them, for when things went tragically off the tracks—which was quite often in a business that could deal out sudden death in the flicker of an eyelash.

Many of the middle-aged and older loggers were, to a man, World War II veterans, and, there in the North-west, they tackled the giant forests like a war zone. They attacked the land as an opponent to be tamed, and they were good at it . . . perhaps a little too good, but they were mere foot soldiers sent by corporate generals to do the gritty groundwork.

Many of the stories in my head are just the gist of things, and often who was involved is lost to time, because I cannot recall the names, and often did not know them in the first place. Loggers died all the time, and often the stories told were a way of passing along wisdom as to what *not* to do, and to always be aware that the unexpected can strike at any time—and that the smart and quick are better suited to survival.

At any rate, this would have been 1969, or so, and Judy and Dick had split up. She got us kids to her mom's in Spokane and went off to Alaska to be a cook in a logging camp. Of course, Dick who was capable of being "Dick" promptly went to Spokane and stole us back, and took us to our aunt in Astoria, Oregon, just to screw with Judy's head while she was in Alaska.

She fixed his wagon by getting married again to Wally Marshall, a big Hupa Indian who was a timber feller, and a great guy in my opinion. And that's how I did fifth grade in Ketchikan—or the first half, anyway—then moved to Annette Island which is governed by the Tsimshian Tribe. Even though Wally was a Hupa he was tribal and worked as a timber feller for the tribe, and a good one as I understand it.

I don't believe Boaz was in school yet, but Lynn and I went to the Coastguard school because we lived in an old Army barracks, converted into rental houses. A restaurant was there, close to the airport, as I recall, because in those days one had to land on Annette Island, then take a small plane to Ketchikan that landed on the water, before they built the big, fancy airport there.

Wally was a tramp logger hailing from Northern California and was raised on the Hupa Reservation, northeast of Eureka, California. They all knew each other from their days in Reedsport, Oregon, which, at one point, was the logging capital on the West Coast, and many a tramp logger passed through that town.

I was thinking on a story that Wally told me once, which I certainly did not appreciate at the time, though it's stuck with me, even if I'm a little shy on details. But, as I experienced life more, it was more and more appreciated for what some of those guys went through in that wild, tough life of their own choosing.

It was before the logging industry had steel towers that they drove to a landing and set up where they chose. I recall them discussing the towers, and it is my thought that this was a transitory time for logging, in many ways, as technology put more men out of work than owls, but I digress.

The way in which they set up a section was to find a big tree in the right spot, go up and top it, then hook up all the cables and yarder, and build a road or, I suppose, railroad in some cases. The guys that climbed and topped were highly specialized individuals, who were at the top of their game. Literately. They would climb and limb up to a certain point that could often be over a hundred feet in the air, and the tree could still be two feet or better in diameter. And where it was situated and how it was rigged was very important, and everything depended on it being done correctly.

Wally could climb and saw, but was not the guy who

did this, though he could if he had to.

He relayed a story of working in some camp where the fellow that did this had climbed and limbed the big spar tree, and, when he cut it off, it barber chaired on him at 90 feet up. It pinned him against the tree with a tremendous amount of pressure on his climbing belt, as the crew looked on horrified!

For those unfamiliar with the term 'barber chair', it's logger lingo for when a tree is cut and does not break off and fall, but some wood is not severed and it goes vertically and splits apart. It can be a very dangerous situation when on the ground, but worse if strapped in, a hundred feet in the air!

When this happened, everyone knew what the outcome would be, including the helpless logger who was still moving. The crew all looked at each other, knowing what must be done, and Wally said, "I'll do it."

And, as he told me, he was a bit stoic. It needed to be done, and it was not going to be easy, both physically and emotionally, I suppose. He gathered a few things for the climb, like chains and straps, and pencils and paper, and got himself rigged up, and up he went until he was face-to-face with his friend. The logger was is in bad shape, and they both knew the end of this story.

Wally got out the pencil and paper, for his buddy to write out a brief note, and will of sorts, as Wally chained the tree, to stop any more barber chair action. He tied his buddy off, to lower him down, and the guy finished his will and told Wally, "Okay, see ya later," before Wally cut him loose.

Wally lowered the body down to the crew.

Then he went down a bit and started re-rigging the tree, because they were still logging. The body was sent to town, and the crew kept working.

These kinds of stories were common, and I do like the funny ones better, but I seem to have lost a few friends lately, both near and far, and the fragility of life is not lost upon me.

So, love your people, and be nice. . . .

WALLY GETS A WOLF

Found a nice picture of Wally Marshall, and of myself as a kid of eleven (or so), when, after Judy's whirlwind romance with him led to her getting hitched, we moved to Ketchikan, Alaska in 1969.

Wally was working in a small logging camp, somewhere in Southeastern Alaska, and they had shut down for a week, or so, in what must have been October. Wally took me out to the camp for a week, and it was great. I got out of school and got to hang out in this little camp as Wally, the cook, and a couple loggers were doing some maintenance work.

Don't recall what they were up to, but I was having a ball, because this little camp was on float logs, in a little bay. When the tide was out, part of the camp sat on the shore.

Every day was a Huck Finn day, as I got to use the boat when the tide was up and wander the shore of the little bay, where one could find whale bones and driftwood of the castle/fort building variety. For a kid, it was a land of giants, and the wildlife was abundant, the fishing great, and it was not hard to keep busy with the imagination factory running on all cylinders. The whole camp rose and fell with the tides, the cook fed me like a pet dog, and I was always hungry.

The loggers were doing logging maintenance stuff and I was an explorer and adventurer of the highest order, with some of the finest companions to accompany me. They were all imaginary, but a pretty good gang!

In the bunkhouse that gently rocked with the tide, they'd talk of logging stories and life in general. I have no recollection of the other loggers, but Wally was great. We went out for halibut, which the cook loved, and that kind of fish is so good. Wally ate the heads and claimed the cheeks were the best part, but I wasn't so sure about that!

I was discovering reading at that time, and there were plenty of books in the bunkhouse, but most of them were a little thick for an eleven-year-old. There were three that I managed to get through, and they have stuck with me, with the first being *Lord of the Flies*, which is a book I reread every few years, to this day. It was, and is, a good guide to human nature. The other two were *The Cross and the Switchblade*, and *Hey, Preach, You're Comin' Through*, which was as much of a juxtaposition from my situation as could be, in hindsight, though I had no idea of what a juxtaposition was, but it was a good read, and probably still is.

Wally would let me shoot the rifle, and it would kick

your ass if you did not hang on correctly. He was patient and thorough in his teaching, as he grew into his step-dad role, made even more challenging with a Backus Cub, I suppose. But he was great, and taught me much in the hunting, fishing, and gutting departments—and how to do them proper. I'm forever grateful.

One fine morning, as we sat in the bunkhouse with the doors open to air it (it could be somewhat odoriferous) the sun was shining and it was nice out, which in Southeastern Alaska, in the fall, is not the norm.

It sure is beautiful country when the sun is upon it, for sure, with the rugged mountains running into the sea, and the rugged shoreline running into the distance, with bald eagles as common as seagulls. They were always busy fishing or eating dead things on the beach, and there was always something floating up that would provide a feast for a hungry eagle, bear, or wolf.

On that particular morning, as we sat looking across the bay, Wally suddenly jumps up and says, "Let's go!" as he grabbed his rifle and headed to the ramp to shore. I was right behind him, as we fast-walked up a logging road that paralleled the shore. We topped a bit of a rise, and about a football field distance away was a big wolf, trotting along. It stopped and looked back, which was its undoing, and Wally got the shot off and dropped him. In those days, there was a $50 bounty on wolves, so we gathered it up and headed back to camp with it.

Thus the picture of me next to it, like I was on safari.

Off with its head to take to town for the bounty, and we saved the tail, which I had for a decade. It might still be at my mom's. We used the body for crab bait and went out into deeper water for that.

When Wally threw it over, it would not sink, and he stabbed it with his knife to let the bloating gas out. I still recall the wanna-puke-smell-of-death that burst out in a noxious wave. Yuck. It promptly sank.

Once back in town, we took the head to the game department, and they slit the ears so we couldn't sell it again, and gave it back to dispose of, after paying. The whole adventure was fun and memorable to this day.

(Above) Wally Marshall
(Below) Me and the wolf

UNDER THE BRIDGE

Sometimes, the exploits of the freewheeling tramp loggers, and the stunts they pulled, just makes one shake their head in wonder—or disbelief!

Often, these guys would get all boozed up and make poor decisions. Most of the time, these poor decisions would be told and retold over the years, to become part of some logger's legend. Booze was ever-present, and a part of the lifestyle in many ways, and alcohol was dealt with in the logging camps with a certain amount of tolerance—so long as it did not interfere with the day-to-day activities necessary to do their job.

As a kid, I did not fully appreciate the gravity of the situations talked about, until much later in life. And, in hindsight, I've realized many suffered from some pretty serious addictions. Often they would sit around drinking whiskey, talking about those that had a "problem," and how it was dealt with when in a camp was funny and often brutal.

When some logger would show up in camp, suffering from withdrawals that would hinder production to the point that it would have to be dealt with, one way or another. Some creative solutions were employed.

Heading back to town was one way, and another was to deal with it in the camp.

I recall stories about them taking such actions as locking up the suffering loggers in a cabin in the camp, until they went through their withdrawals to the point of being able to work productively. Some of the more severe cases involved the logger going "snakey," or delirium tremens, in which they would see snakes and other hallucinations, like a hippie on bad acid!

But it was part of things, and it's impossible to judge folks by today's standards, I suppose. Booze was a part of the culture then, and still is. It's just the way it was, and factors into many of these stories. When looking at things through a kid's eyes, it was part of the "normal."

One will fight devils along their path—just never let the bastards get the upper hand.

At any rate, enough with the sermon and on to the story that bubbled up. If memory serves, this involved a couple tramp loggers relocating to another place to live, and one did not know it was moving day.

I am guessing this took place somewhere in Oregon in the 1950s. Dick Robbins was staying in a camper trailer, at a trailer court, and Poky Twight was bunking with him at the time. They were working at some logging job in the area, maybe Reedsport, and Dick Robbins had gotten fired from his job and went to the bar to get shitfaced, which was a method of dealing with stress. He was pissed off he had gotten fired, but it was not long before he had another job and could start the next day, up the coast some. So, Dick Robbins said, "No problem —I'll get my trailer and head up today."

He hooked up the trailer, after sitting in the bar for hours, and he headed out in a hurry to make it up the coast. While driving under a little railroad bridge, on the way out of town, he either misjudged or did not pay any attention to the sign about how tall a vehicle would fit under.

As he went under, the truck fit just fine but the trailer was just a smidge too tall, and it kinda almost fit —but not quite. So, he just backed up, gave it the peddle, and made it almost through. So, he backed up again and gave it hell.

He burst out the other side, and off he went to the new job, with what I am sure would be some roof repairs going on in the near future. But it was summer, so worry about that later, I suppose.

When he got to where he was going and parked, he went back to the trailer and was greeted by Poky Twight, who had been sleeping in the trailer when it got hooked up. He'd woke up when the trailer started moving, and he said he really came to when the bridge indecent happened, as he was thrown out of the bunk and then tossed around pretty good when the back-and-forth of scraping the trailer under the bridge was underway.

As the story went, he was challenged with getting out when the bridge indecent was ongoing, because of the big logging truck tire that Dick Robbins had inside, so no one would steal it. That tire rolled around pretty good, and Poky was not a big man so it was quite a ride for him!

Since Dick Robbins had decided to relocate, apparently Poky did as well, and got a job straight away as they settled into the new place.

HERMAN SILVERS'
WINDOW DISPLAY

Herman Silvers was an Indian fellow from Canada, and back in the day, as I understand it, there was a lot of interchangeability with Canadian loggers. But a law was passed at some point that put a stop to it because of Americans taking Canadian work, or visa versa. I'm unsure of how that worked, but there seemed to be a few Canadians in that loose group of creatures known as tramp loggers, and Herman's name is one I heard as a kid.

Would have been about 1964, is my thought, and the Backus family (pre-Boaz) was moving from Seaside, Oregon, or Gearheart to be more specific, to Aberdeen, Washington, and there were always timber tramp types around. Herman was helping with the move and was heading to that area for a job, so he loaded a truck full of stuff and sent it north. Uncle Pat McVay was visiting his sister Judy from Spokane, at the time, and he and Herman were to take the truck.

At that time, the bridge across the Columbia River

was under construction, and there was a ferry. I clearly recall seeing the bridge being worked on, from the ferry, and I think that the ferry ended up on Puget Sound, after it was built.

At any rate, when they were set to depart, Dick said to Herman, "Let Pat drive." Pat was fourteen, and he said Herman was terrified the whole time as he learned a new skill!

As they settled into the Grays Harbor area, Herman was known to frequent the smoke shop in downtown Aberdeen, as did many a tramp. It was a 24-hour joint that had a restaurant and a bar that closed at 2 A.M., and Herman headed out of there one late night, or early morning, heading to where he was staying.

He had stopped to admire a nice camping display, in the window of a sporting goods store down the block from the bar, and was of thought, I suppose, that it sure looked comfortable. He decided to take a leak in the doorway, before moving on, and he leaned on the door for support (as anyone who has taken a leak after leaving a bar knows, it is a good idea to steady oneself.)

Lo and behold, when he leaned on the door, it turned out to be open, because whoever locked up did not actually lock the door. And Herman, being a resourceful fellow who had a long walk ahead of him, just went right into the window display and crawled into that nice sleeping bag.

And that's where the cops found him in the morning!

GEORGE HIDES UNDER A ROCK

The memory dredge is a bit slow this morning, but a George Broulett story seemed to come up somewhat intact.

George was one of the younger tramps that were full-on into the game, and he logged from Oregon to Southeastern Alaska. He was an Indian fellow from Haines, Alaska, and he was living in Juneau, around this time. I recall him telling the story, and while it's not word-for-word, it's as I remember it—with my particular twist.

George said that he was performing a bit of a criminal act, as he was stealing fuel from some contractor outside of town. The place was on the rocky seashore, and while he was performing this illicit deed it was well after dark—as many illicit deeds are performed that way.

George was low on funds and gas, from the sounds of it, and he said that in the act of redistributing some fuel, he didn't have his wheels with him. (It was possibly out of fuel, somewhere close, thus leading to his nefarious solution.)

At any rate, as George was transferring fluids the shop owner rolled in and put George in a bit of a situation, because there was no cover or place to hide in a hurry, and this fellow might resort to gunplay to halt a poor logger down on his luck. George knew this could be a possibility because pissed-off shop owners had been known to fire warning shots straight at whoever had been caught red-handed!

George calculated his odds, dropped everything, and bolted over the edge of the shore onto the rocky beach. The shopkeeper must have got a glimpse of his fleeing behind, and, as George made his way up the beach at a pretty good clip, he said it did not seem like but a minute that a big, very bright searchlight began probing the beach behind him!

He said he went to the edge of the water and laid down flat since he could see the light moving around, as they looked for this miscreant who dared to borrow some fuel. As he laid in the gravel, he grabbed a big flat rock that was handy, and as the light worked its way up toward him, he held it up in front of his face, to blend in with the rest of the beach. It must have worked, because he said that after a while they gave up and he walked down the beach to escape.

He said they did not give up right away, and as he lay there not moving he had been getting concerned because the tide had been coming in, and it was cold. . . .

CHEST HAIR-PULLING CONTEST

Dirty Dick Backus was a pretty ballsy individual, of this there was no doubt, judging from some of his escapades. I have put down some on paper, but would also guess there are plenty of stories I will never know about. But this story has been in the family lore since I can remember, and I've heard it many times. Judy has told it more than once, because she was there, and still laughs in the telling.

This would have taken place in Portland, Oregon, early in their relationship. The early 1960s, or so. They went out for a night of revelry at some rough, drinking establishment in town, that would have been full of the kind of characters one would have expected in a place like that.

There was a great, big hairy logger in there that was whiskey-talking on his ability to do many feats. One thing that Dick did not suffer from was fear, and he could hold his own in fisticuffs if it came to that. But he was pretty sharp at using his wit to dance out of a situation, when he could—which was more often than not.

Judy said that after a while of listening to this fellow blather on (and she said he was a very large guy, maybe 6' 4", and 250 pounds), Dick challenged him to a chest hair-pulling contest!

Judy said this guy said, "Hell yes!" pulled his shirt up to expose a chest full of hair that looked like a bear rug, and told Dick, "Go ahead!"

Dick grabbed a handful of fur and twisted a good-sized patch right out of the guy's chest. The fellow winced in pain as Dick ripped it out, and then said "Okay! Now my turn!"

And Dirty Dick From Pistol Crick stood back and took a stance, so the crowd could get a good look at the payback, and the big guy got ready to balance the books, so to speak.

Dick pulled his shirt up to his chin, and he had no hair on his chest. At all!

The big guy took one look at the hairless chest, threw his head back, and burst out laughing. He said "You win!" and bought Dick a drink. . . .

DICK SEES A SASQUATCH

This particular tale would have taken place in the late 1980s, and Dick was living in his van and running his trap line (so to speak) by staying with me, then Lynn, then Boaz, and, now and again, Uncle Pat.

He would stay a while, until he drove you crazy with his carefree lifestyle, then move on after a bit . . . but he'd show back up two months later, with a couple sacks of groceries and a bottle of wine. We were always glad to see him since he always was a happy guy who liked to cook, drink wine, and tell stories—of which there seemed to be a bottomless well.

I heard many, but cannot seem to recall them at will —I remember them as best as I am able when they pop to the surface.

Dick was still at the edge of the tramp logger world, to where he could pretty much always get a job driving a log truck in a camp, and that summer as he drove us batshit crazy at times, while we tried to do adulting and he would drink wine and point out what *we* should do!

He got an opportunity to go to Alaska for a job driving a log truck in the southeast. I don't know where, exactly, but he ended up in the hospital in Sitka when a small log fell off the truck and smacked him a good one.

He even bought me the book *Alaska*, by James Michener, when he got out of the hospital where Mr. Michener was having a book signing. He missed having it signed by the author by a couple hours.

James Michener would always move to wherever he was going to write about and live there as he wrote the book. He was there three years, and Dick missed him by an hour.

At any rate, before he could get to Alaska, he needed to come up with the money to get there. We were so eager for him to go to work we raised $800 for a ticket, in about a day, and off he went. Must have been around May, I am thinking.

By summer's end, he was back on the island with a nice settlement check, ready for a winter on his trapline. And would show up with four sacks of groceries and two bottles of wine.

Be a couple years, or so, I reckon, and we were talking about Sasquatches and things like that. He told a story about when he was up in Alaska on that truck driving job, and he and the loader operator were up on a clearcut, with a fine view of the water and mountains, at the end of the day.

They were leaning on the truck, shooting the shit, when they noticed a disturbance in the water in a little bay. It was far enough off they could see the water splashing about, but could not see what was making the disturbance. They thought it was a sea lion, or something like that, and kept an eye on it while continuing the bullshit session.

Dick said that whatever it was, was working its way toward the shore. It was still far enough away that they still couldn't see clearly what it was . . . but it was splashing about quite a bit.

He said that, as whatever was splashing about was headed straight towards shore, they both stopped talking and were watching the water. And, when whatever it was got to shallow water, it stood up and walked into the woods!

He and the loader operator looked at each other with a *what the fuck?*

I said, "I'd never heard this one before," and he said, "Hell no! Everyone would think we were crazy, so we never told anyone, because maybe it was a bear. . . . But it stood up and walked upright!

It would be fair to say he was not a tall tale sort of fellow, but could certainly lie when he needed to— mostly when he plead "Not guilty, your honor."

Who knows what they saw?

CHAINSAWS, AND IVAN BACUS

The memory dredge has been bouncing around some, and you never know what will come up. This time it was chainsaw carving contests (the early ones especially—they all have some kind of backstory to them,) and how they originated, grew, cross-pollinated, and, layer-by-layer, have become some damn fine entertainment!

This particular art form—which is the age-old art of woodcarving, but on steroids—is just one more example of crafty humans adapting technology to their own purposes, and experimenting with *not* using a tool for its intended purpose. Over a span of time, it evolved into what we see today in the carver world!

Carving bars, small, lightweight chainsaws, chain breaks . . . there are so many aspects that are taken for granted these days, that make me smile at some of the complaints I hear. I suppose it's a simple analogy, but when we were kids we walked uphill both ways to get to school, in the snow, barefoot! Today, you can just get on a warm bus with good heaters and get dropped off at the door!

So, let us start with the chainsaw itself. Not to get too far into the weeds on its origins, I will tell a story told to me by someone who was right there at the cross-over times, which is certainly tied to the timber industry. It is my thought that there was logging all over the world, for sure, ever since humans figured out it was nice to have fire and shelter, to what we see today.

In the Pacific Northwest, back in the day, the big timber looked inexhaustible, and those who could get it down, to where it had to go, fastest, were the ones that moved up the food chain. It's quite possible we were a little too good at it, but folks wanted to live in houses, so waddya gonna do?

Efficiency is less work and more production. A great cook would not give up their gas stove for a charcoal hearth, or a writer give up their keyboard for an inkwell and quill—if so, throw that darn cell phone out, right now!

I'm going in a different direction than when I started out, but I do that all the time since I am not a trained writer; I just write down what leaks out at the moment.

Sedro-Woolley, Washington, has one of the best chainsaw carving contests around. It was started when Rocky MacArthur went to the big Westport contest, came home, and started one there in 1996. While I missed the first one, I have been there for most of them, since then, and along the way I was introduced to Ivan

Bacus.

He was a lifelong resident of that area, and as a young man was a bit of a tramp logger himself. Each year, after we had gotten to know each other, I would be carving away and I would see him walk by. I would al-ways stop carving to say, "Why hello, Mr. Bacus," and he would smile and say, "Why hello, Mr. Backus."

Our names being spelled different, but sounding the same, made it seem like we were related, but no. We had great conversations, as he was well into his 80s at that point, and had led a full life. This story of his has stuck with me.

In 1949 he had been working down near Mapleton, Oregon, just out of Florence, and they were logging up these steep draws. The fellers had gone through, and fell the trees as best as they could, all with axe and whipsaw, in those days.

After the fellers did their business, the buckers would work the section. These guys would cut the logs to the proper lengths, all with whipsaws, so the yarder could then yard them out of the woods, and stack them up for the trucks or trains to haul to the mills.

Mr. Bacus said it would take them two weeks to buck up all the logs into manageable lengths, and time was money, as much then as it is now, and efficiency was as important to the bean counters, then as now. Do it smarter = less man hours = less costs = more profits; kinda like those self-ordering kiosks in McDonald's, I suppose.

Mr. Bacus talked the boss into buying a chainsaw, which was a very new tool on the market in 1949, but two guys could pack one into the brush with a can of gasoline and cut logs so efficiently, that two guys went through that timber in two days instead of two weeks!

He said that within the month, the whole crew had chainsaws.

He has passed on, but, if memory serves, Peter Wiant and I have that story on film from an interview with Mr. Bacus, when he came down to Westport in the late 1990s

I think that technology and hydraulic power have put more loggers out of work than any owl or regulation.

PHOTOGRAPHS
AND MEMORIES

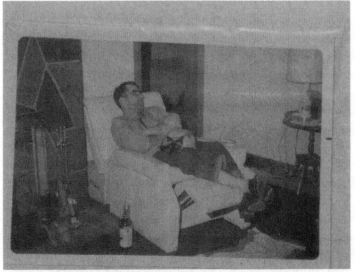

Emil Williams, famed hooktender in the tramp logger world,
passed out in a chair with a half gallon of whiskey ready to go,
should he wake up thirsty.

In Ketchikan, in the late 1960s, Emil took a cab somewhere and the
cab driver was of Japanese decent. He took his pistol out and asked
the driver where he was December 7, 1941!

A gaggle of tramp logger all dressed up. From left to right, Pokey Twight, a little Steve Backus, Faybell and Roger Crum, then a young Dirty Dick Backus holding a beer, his faithful German Shepherd Lobo, my young Mom behind Lobo, Pack Sack Louie to her right, and his wife, Jane, to her left. . . . A rough bunch, I assure you!

The Oxbow Tavern in Humtulips, early 1970s.

Dirty Dick Backus in his truck, mid 1950s.
(See the cover for the colorized photo.)

The author, of course!

Dirty Dick Backus well into requirement. He really liked wine in a box because, when he was done, he could blow the bag up and make a little pillow. This was taken at ten o'clock in the morning!

My uncle Pat McVay who logged one summer when he stayed with us in 1969. He was not a tramp logger, but because of us he was on the edge of it. Besides, I like the picture.

It is the intention of both publisher and author, to further elaborate upon the stories told in this volume. Whether that be in later expanded editions, or new volumes of tall (yet true) tales, Sprague River Publishing looks forward to more from Steve Backus.

—*Joseph Bergstrom,*
Sprague River Publishing

This novel was typeset using a combination of
ADOBE MINION PRO
&
ITC Serif Gothic

STEVE BACKUS was born in Spokane, Washington, and raised in Western Washington, with many moves from Southeastern Alaska to Southern Oregon as his dad followed the logging industry up and down the Coast. He spent much of this time in Humptulips, Washington, located in the big timber country of Grays Harbor County, and was influenced by the many bigger-than-life characters who were known as tramp loggers.

He is a second-generation chainsaw carver, following after his mother who was a pioneer in that peculiar art that grew out of the timber industry. He now resides on an island in Puget Sound/Salish Sea and has been a full-time chainsaw carver for more than 40 years.

Made in United States
Troutdale, OR
12/09/2024

25762155R00082